The Bill

The Bill

JOHN BURKE

Thames Mandarin

A Thames Mandarin Paperback

THE BILL

First published in Great Britain 1985
by Methuen London
This edition published 1989
Reprinted 1991, 1992
by Mandarin Paperbacks
Michelin House, 81 Fulham
Road, London SW3 6RB
in association with
Thames Television International Ltd
149 Tottenham Court Road, London W1P 9LL

Mandarin is an imprint
of the Octopus Publishing Group
a division of Reed International Books Ltd

Novel Copyright © 1985 John Burke
Television scripts copyright © 1984 and 1985
Geoff McQueen and Barry Appleton

A CIP catalogue record
for this book is available
from the British Library

ISBN 0 7493 0277 1

Printed in Great Britain
by Cox & Wyman Ltd, Reading, Berks.

One

The voice on the car radio babbled on, pouring out a whole load of cheerful garbage. All right for him, tucked away in his cosy studio with his turntable and his tea and biscuits, nicely sheltered from the tough old real old world outside. Nobody ought to be that cheerful at half past five in the morning. Even the sunlight, pale and shifty along the edge of the railway viaduct and on rusty sheets of corrugated iron dangling from a derelict warehouse, knew better than to look cheerful.

Sergeant Bob Cryer stopped for a red light and looked both ways. It was a waste of time really, with not another car in sight; but policemen had to set a good example. All nice and quiet at the moment. A bit too early for today's crop of villains to be out on the streets, and a bit too late for whatever some of them might have been up to last night. It all looked nice and innocent and tranquil. Not much chance of it staying that way for long.

Cryer crossed the junction and swung into the covered yard of Sun Hill police station; slowed, swerved; and swore.

Trouble showed signs of starting already. An ambulance with its rear doors open was backed up to the ramp. As Cryer pulled into a vacant parking slot, two ambulance men emerged from the building and edged a stretcher smoothly between the doors. The police surgeon stood in the station doorway and watched. His face was drawn with tiredness – and something else, something more sombre.

'Morning, doc.' Cryer made his way across the yard. 'What's all this, then?'

'Drink drive case.'

5

'Messed himself up?'

'No.'

'What's with the ambulance, then?'

Dr Grimshaw's lips were tight. 'Threw a fit in his cell. Epilepsy.'

'Oh, great. How is he now?'

'Not too good, I'm afraid.'

Grimshaw followed on into the ambulance, and the doors swung shut. Cryer sighed and turned along the clattering, echoing corridor into the nick to face whatever the day might bring. A flurry of good-mornings, the usual chatter of somebody having an argument halfway up the concrete staircase, and then the duty sergeant was saying, 'Am I glad to see you!'

Obviously it had been one of those nights: which often meant it was going to be one of those days as well.

Cryer flicked over a leaf of the night book. 'What's the score?'

'Three in the men's cell and one in the women's. No, sorry: two in the men's. We just had one carted away to hospital.'

'Yeah, I just saw the wagon pull out. The quack was looking well worried.'

'Dropped a right clanger, didn't he.' It was a statement, not a question.

The sergeant went on to explain, curtly and wasting no time. There never was time to waste on a lot of talk in here.

Two men on the beat had found an odd type parked up on the pavement in High Street at three in the morning. He was slumped over the wheel, with the engine still running. When Hollis and Burton opened the door, the smell of drink nigh took their helmets off. The chap was dead to the world so they brought him in. The duty sergeant hadn't liked the look of him and called out the doctor, who was none too pleased to be dragged out of bed. After giving the man the once-over he said he was just drunk. The usual routine: leave him in a cell to cool off until morning.

'Then about twenty minutes ago the guy throws a wobbler. Ain't never seen nothing like it.'

'No comebacks on us?' asked Cryer sharply.

'No. All done by the book. The doc might have some explaining to do, though.'

Cryer thought that was all too likely. Grimshaw had looked pretty sick.

He turned his attention to sorting out parade sheets. Even at first glance a familiar pattern emerged, carrying over from yesterday and from last week and the week before that . . . and on its way, you could bet, into the far distant future.

In the parade room he made a quick appraisal of the faces he knew as well as he knew the streets and alleys and doorways of Wapping. It was a tough manor, and if you weakened it could get right on top of you. But after twenty years Bob Cryer was still a fighter, trained the hard way and proud of it. He wanted his team to be fighters, too – but skilful fighters, knowing when to punch and when to shadow box and when to back away and play it very, very clever. It was from not being clever enough that he had once, long ago, had his own nose smashed in, and then had it repaired to look like the beak of an aggressive parrot. Not many people risked making comments on that, though.

PC Litten looked fagged out, even though the day was only just beginning. Maybe he had been up half the night chasing some bird; or maybe swotting for the next step in his hoped-for transfer to CID. The lad was getting just a bit too pushy in that direction: too much elbow and not enough know-how.

One of the girls looked unhappy – WPC Ackland, still in a state over some messed-up love affair. With Litten, Cryer suspected. Now he had other interests. She'd learn.

Young Carver's smooth, scrubbed face was bright and wide awake. But was he going to be tough enough? Some of these youngsters from the police college at Hendon were keen on the job and smart on the theory, but often lacked that real instinct – call it killer instinct, call it just plain bloody stamina, call it what you liked – the boil-up of intuition and slogging persistence that led you in the right direction and kept you moving. On the whole he thought Carver would make it. Not right away, but he'd go through the mill and in the end he'd make it.

'Right,' said Cryer.

Two of the men cleared their throats. The girls looked earnest and attentive. Duplicated sheets rustled as they were turned over and studied. At the side of the room, Detective Inspector Galloway propped his feet on the rung of a neighbouring chair and yawned ostentatiously. Roy Galloway always made a big act of letting the uniform branch know what he thought of them.

Ignoring him, Cryer briskly outlined the main duties for the day. A faint moan drifted back to him when he dragged up the old trouble, the disease they all knew about but could never quite cure. It was like a plague, transmitted from one street to another, checked in one back alley only to break out again halfway across the manor. Pickpockets were out in force again. Everyone with beats covering or crossing the High Street had to keep a beady eye out. There was every indication that the firm was the same as one operating on this patch about three months ago. Descriptions were sketchy, but there seemed to be at least three in the regular team: the usual pusher, the catcher, and of course the dipper. Also there were hints that one of the team was a blonde, good-looking woman who specialized in the pushing when the chosen victim was a male.

'Showing lots of cleavage, eh?' offered PC Edwards hopefully.

Cryer glared. 'Keep your attention on wandering hands, not the other bits. And now, sheet 4. Theft from vehicles. Figures are up again this month. Maybe now that the kids are going back to school there'll be a bit of a drop. Just the same, I want you on your toes. Pull anyone you see acting a bit sussy around the various car parks. But be careful. I don't want a stack of complaints from the public about over-zealous policing, understand?'

They nodded and murmured. Galloway's shoes scraped restlessly on the chair rung.

'OK, then.' Cryer glanced at the clock. 'Now, the last item on page 8. Crime Watch – which means breaking and entering. It's a month since this operation has been in effect, and I can tell you now that figures for last month are lower.' He allowed himself a faint smile. They waited for it like puppies grateful for a stroke and words of encouragement. 'However' – the rasp came back into his voice – 'I'd point out it's still early days. Too early for us to be patting ourselves on the back. Right. Before you hit the streets, Inspector Galloway from CID is here. He'd like a few words on the subject.'

Shoulders slumped as Roy Galloway unhitched himself from his chair and sauntered forward. His sandy hair and high complexion seemed drained of colour this morning, like someone who had spent a sleepless night – and not for any fun he got out of it. One thumb went automatically into the waistband of his trousers. His nose wrinkled as if it hurt him to be here.

'Thank you, sergeant.' The word sounded like an insult. 'Now. You should all have a copy of my memo on a particular kind of screw-in, break-in, MO, yes?' As the papers rustled yet again, he snapped out: 'You all know what an MO is, eh? Edwards?'

Taffy Edwards smiled up guilelessly. 'Medical orderly, sir?'

'Modus operandi,' snarled Galloway. 'Latin.'

'Oh.' Taffy looked as if it would have made little difference even if it had been in Welsh.

'Make a mental note of this particular MO. Pay special attention to recent double-glazed properties with no sign of forced entry.' Cryer noticed that PC Litten was hanging on every word, staring attentively at Galloway, advertising himself as real on-the-ball CID material. It turned your stomach. 'If you get called out to a screw-in and it bears a close resemblance,' said Galloway, 'I want to know. And double-quick. Get straight on the wire to your guv'nor, then after that don't touch a thing. Stay on the scene until my team arrive. Got it?'

Cryer said: 'Thank you, inspector. All right, that's it. On your bikes.'

As they squeezed out into the corridor and their footsteps rattled off in different directions, Roy Galloway stood beside the doorway watching the dispersal with a curl of the lip. The skinny little sod knew at least ten different ways of twisting his face into expressions of scorn, thought Cryer.

'Didn't have to sit through all that lot really, did I, Robert? Didn't really expect quite such a production.'

'Listen,' said Cryer slowly and deliberately. 'I brief my officers in a tried and tested fashion. If you think I'm going to turn it arse about face just to please you, you have another think coming.'

'Thanks for nothing.'

'And another thing. Don't come in here treating my lot like they're a bunch of schoolkids, right?'

'Yes, headmaster.'

Cryer brushed past him and stamped along to the front office. The switchboard was buzzing into life. All you had to do was wait, and it would all happen: kids would go missing, goods would go missing, someone would clobber his wife and someone else would clobber half the punters in the park, the complaints would come screeching in . . . and out there his boys and girls would spread out, hunt, call in or be called in, keep on the move for as many hours as the day had in it. They were like healthy corpuscles, he had once thought after a compulsory lecture by some visiting expert from Forensic, rushing about on the alert through a very murky bloodstream.

Most of the time, though, Cryer didn't think in any such terms. He just tackled what came, on its own merits: if merits was the right word, which it very rarely was.

He glanced at the calendar. His next leave was a long way off. And his wife said he was a misery and a fidget when he was away from the nick for more than a couple of days, anyway.

From the switchboard June Ackland said: 'Sarge . . .'

The day was getting under way.

Two

Early shoppers were making erratic lunges over zebra cross-
ings, blundering into men on their way to and from the
riverside wharves and warehouses. The inevitable idlers
shuffled from one shop front to another or lounged in the
doorways of snack bars and newsagents, squeezing empty
Coke tins into distorted shapes. Why, Jimmy Carver wondered, did folk like that come out at this time of the morning
when there was nothing to do once they had got here?

Heads turned as the two constables plodded past. A group
of youths in jeans and studded jackets allowed themselves a
knowing sneer: contemptuous, but not *too* contemptuous.
Then the heads turned the other way as a girl with puce hair
wriggled her way towards an office block with a faded sign
offering two upper floors to let. Carver watched her bottom
as it disappeared up a brief flight of steps. At least it was
doing something to brighten up the morning.

Taffy Edwards laughed. 'You know what, Jimbo? I reckon
June Ackland quite fancies you.'

'Come off it.'

'I been watching her. In the parade room, the way she
keeps giving you the eye.'

'Get away. You're winding me up.'

'It's not a wind-up, honest. You ought to get in there,
you'll score first time.'

Carver felt himself going pink. All that sort of talk round
the station, and the ribbing in the canteen, it was all harmless
enough, but still he didn't go for it. All right, so once or twice
during morning briefings he had glanced at June Ackland's
profile, and rather liked the line of her neck below that crisp

12

blonde hair. And once or twice when she had been bending forward over the switchboard and had caught his eye she had half smiled: but it was a pitying sort of smile, the opposite of a come-on, half telling him he'd never be lively enough and half telling him to stop gawping. Anyway, she was still getting over some kind of bust-up with Dave Litten, and Jimmy Carver was none too sure he fancied one of Litten's leftovers.

No, that was pushing it too far. There was more to her than that. Maybe the thing had bust up because she didn't fancy anyone that crude. Good for her. Maybe when it had all blown over she'd smile in a different way, and they'd both be good and ready, and he, Jimmy Carver, with a lot more experience under his belt . . .

Hastily he said: 'I wouldn't get involved with anyone in the job. So scrub round it.'

'Oh, very commendable, Jimbo. Very professional.' Taffy grinned. 'Come on, I'll treat you to a bit of breakfast.'

'Breakfast? But we've only been on for half an hour.'

He found himself talking to Taffy's retreating back, and had to quicken his pace to catch up.

They turned down a narrow alley with a rich complement of dustbins, empty boxes, cardboard cartons, and a stench that had been around for a long time and was unlikely to go away in a hurry. A hot breath of bacon and chips belched out of an extractor in the wall. Taffy reached a grimy back door, and opened it with a dramatic flourish.

'This'll put some lead in your pencil, boyo.'

The draught of warm air and breakfast odours enveloped them. A girl in a flimsy blue dress was poised above a table in the act of laying two plates of sausages and beans in front of a couple of workmen. Quite an act it was, too. The men were more interested in a page of racing tips than in the girl. Carver wouldn't have been if he had been sitting where they were. The girl's dress was cut low, and for two very good reasons.

Taffy nudged him. 'See what I mean?'

13

Jimmy Carver saw.

Then the girl looked up and said, 'Cor, look what the tide's just washed up,' but smiled, and then got a good look at Carver and smiled a bit more.

Something came between them. It was a large woman who had long since given up wearing skimpy, low-cut little dresses.

'You're a bit early this morning,' she said to Taffy Edwards, and then, questioningly: 'A new face, eh?'

'Annie, meet Jimbo. But watch him. Quite an eye for the ladies, young Jimbo. Jimbo, meet Annie – does the best breakfast in the whole of London.'

Carver fumbled the helmet off his head and took the opportunity of edging to one side. This way the view was a whole lot better. Gathering up a pile of dirty plates and swinging towards the counter flap, the girl paused and let her dress slip, writhing one shoulder so that it slithered just so many inches and then was miraculously stopped.

Annie folded her arms across a bosom which was ample but no longer alluring. 'Carol, where'd you hide them tins of beans what came in yesterday?'

'D'yer look in the back?' Carol's voice was not as sleek and inviting as the rest of her. Carver flinched as the volume was turned up. 'Course you didn't.'

She stormed on through the open flap.

Jimmy Carver had already eaten before leaving his digs this morning, as he always did. He made do with a cup of tea while Taffy chomped his way through two bacon rolls. It was another chunk of experience – learning about a café like this, and watching his mate's lips begin to glisten with bacon fat. Taffy's mouth was in fact good and full when his radio crackled into life and WPC Ackland's voice came over. 'Uniform Oscar to one-oh-one. Over.' Taffy gulped, tucked a wedge of bacon and crust behind his upper molars, and acknowledged. 'Proceed to rear car park, supermarket, the High Street, tunnel end,' came the instruction. 'Report of suspicious person tampering with parked vehicles.'

Taffy pushed the plate away, washed the last mouthful down with tea, and was on his feet. 'Come on, Jimbo. Just down the road.'

They burst out of the back door into the alley as Carver struggled to get his helmet on straight.

The car park was on a rough patch of ground which was beaten hard in summer but like a marsh on a wet wintry day. Drivers who got here first made use of arches in the high building which cast a shadow over the site – arches which had once been wine cellars before the upper storeys facing out on to the main road had been expanded into a supermarket and shopping precinct. Others stayed outside and by the end of each day accumulated rust-red smears of soot and oily smut over their roofs and bonnets. Carver and Edwards paused at the head of the shallow slope down on to the main parking lot, and surveyed the bumpy surface. Nothing moved. Cautiously they went down and split up, Carver circling round to the west end and making his way back beside a row of cars close to the towering brick wall. Taffy reported arrival into his PR, cut off, and carefully closed in from the opposite end.

Carver reached the darkly gaping mouth of one of the arches. Something glinted and then was gone as he took another step or two.

He eased in under the overhang and tried to adjust his eyes to the sudden twilight.

It came into focus: a car radio below the partly open door of a pricey little coupé, and, half kicked under the car, a briefcase and a camera.

Someone had been interrupted by their arrival. Whoever he was, he couldn't be far away.

Carver stooped for a closer examination, then swiftly straightened up. Not ten feet away, from between a Rover and a rusty Ford Granada, a man broke cover and began to leg it across the car park towards the exit.

'Taffy!'

They scrambled between two lines of cars, found an open

patch, converged between two more ranks and saw their quarry racing up the ramp. Carver's breath rasped in his throat. His first bit of luck, his first big chance: he couldn't fluff it, wasn't going to, *couldn't.*

'Stop – police!'

The man, going like the clappers, knew without looking round that they were gaining on him. He swerved away from the exit, went over the low wall, and sprinted like a mad thing across the road and towards the alley behind Annie's café.

Carver could hear him whimpering. Well out of condition, this one. He wasted none of his own breath, not even on another shout. He was gaining, and Taffy was close behind. He aimed to crowd the man, forcing him over towards the line of dustbins and teetering boxes.

Right. Now. Carver braced himself to make a long, wild leap on to the fugitive's back.

The door of the café opened: opened outwards.

There was no way either of them could stop. The man went head-on into the edge of the door and was flung aside. Carver took the full force of the rebound, and the two of them piled up in a thrashing heap on the rubbish bins, while the door thudded back to the accompaniment of a loud crash and a scream of rage from inside.

'Jimbo.' Taffy came panting to a halt. 'Jimbo, you all right? Like a bloody greyhound, I couldn't . . .'

His voice trailed away. He heaved Carver to his feet, then stood back. A yellow mess began to drip from Carver's shoulder down the front of his tunic. Taffy seemed happier to risk tackling their quarry; but the man had had enough. 'Awright, awright.' He waved a weary hand in defeat, and let Taffy prop him against the wall.

The door opened again, more cautiously this time. Annie's head came round it.

'What the bloody hell's going on?'

'It's all right, Annie. It's us. You all right then, love?'

'You put the fear of God up our Carol. Miracle she ain't broke her neck, the way that door slammed shut.'

Carol forced her way past, out into the alley. She was plastered from head to foot in what had presumably started life as three large helpings of beans, sausages and tomatoes in a great deal of juice – not to mention a liberal helping of brown sauce which had appeared from somewhere.

'I'll bloody kill whoever . . . I'm telling you, I'll kill 'em . . . I'll . . .'

Carver risked a friendly smile.

Annie contemplated the crumpled crates and one of the dustbins which had been knocked sideways.

'I told you. Them bins should have been emptied two days ago, not left here like this. And them eggs . . . I told you they was rotten, don't say I didn't tell you.'

Carver did not need to be told. His own nose had already settled that point. Helplessly he dabbed at the sticky mess on his uniform. Taffy kept his distance, beginning to smile; could not help the smile broadening; and Annie was cackling, doubling up, wiping her eyes with the hem of her none too savoury apron.

Dripping and demoralized, Carver stared beseechingly at Carol.

Bang went that daydream, anyway. Short and sweet. Only not what you'd call sweet. He had heard of having egg on your face, but had never thought of what the real thing would be like. Fat chance of even a cup of tea on these premises from now on.

A flash of colour slid to a halt across the end of the alley. One of the mobile patrols, alerted by June Ackland, had arrived to help, or at least to pick up the pieces. When they saw the pieces, the two men tried to nod sympathetically. The gesture was spoilt when they began to look and then snigger like Taffy Edwards.

'Well,' said the driver heartlessly as he carted them all away, 'you can't make an omelette without breaking something or other. A pity it had to be such a ripe vintage, though.'

17

Sergeant Cryer was waiting for them to return. His eyes welcomed them; his nose had second thoughts; his mouth twitched, and he turned away.

The duty sergeant took the arrested man and his two captors into the charge room. Whatever he thought about the grade or condition of the eggs adorning PC Carver's uniform, he said nothing. What he did say something about was the abject, sly little creep sitting behind the table. He said it loud and clear and kept hammering on about it, because it was too obvious that the little rat was getting his nerve back and deciding to play it all cocky and clever.

'I wanna see the CID.' The expression was smug enough to make Carver and Edwards uneasy. What did the grubby little crook know? *Who* did he know? It had to be a con, said Carver fervently to himself. 'A DI,' whined the man, his right eye beginning to twitch and blink. 'Or a DCI. No one lower.'

'You what? You got some chances, pal. You,' said Sergeant Penny weightily, 'are in dead lumber.'

At this moment Sergeant Cryer chose to join them. He winked approvingly at Carver, who ought to have felt flattered but was in no mood to wink, even respectfully, at anyone.

Penny said: 'Bob, this rubbish won't give his name, and is now demanding – demanding, mark you – to see someone from CID.'

'Let me make one phone call, and I'll front up me name.' The twitching eyes were bleary but knowing.

'Games ain't going to do you no good, son. Now, what's your name?'

'I've told you – '

'That's right. Go on telling me. *Name*?'

There was a pause, then: 'Mickey.'

'Now we're being sensible.' Sergeant Penny scribbled on the sheet before him. 'Michael . . .?'

'Mouse. Mickey Mouse.'

Penny went faintly mauve around his ear lobes. Cryer loomed behind him and said: 'Now look – '

'I gotta talk to CID. Leave it out, will yer? You just don't know, but *they* do. Tell the CID.'

'Belt up.' Cryer stepped forward, found himself too close to Carver, and winced. 'Honest, you pen an' ink, son. Go get yourself cleaned up.'

Jimmy Carver was only too glad to make his escape. In the locker room he showered and changed into a clean shirt, rinsing the old one and flicking water towards Taffy Edwards.

Taffy shook his head tolerantly. 'I remember my first collar. Great feeling, right?'

'Just doing our job.'

'Hark at Mr Modest! Don't try and con me, boyo. I was there, remember? I saw your face after it was all done. Pleased as punch you were.'

Carver felt the warmth glowing up inside him. All right, it was true. He had to admit it: he felt well chuffed. There had been panic for a moment, a moment that had seemed a ruddy lifetime, a moment, or ten minutes, or fifty flaming years, when he had thought the bastard might get away. But he'd done it. Got him.

'My,' said Taffy, 'but you can run. I'll say that for you.'

Carver flung more water at him. Taffy twisted a tap on, put his thumb under it, and directed a jet back.

'Have we done?' It was Sergeant Cryer. 'There's an empty beat out there just yearning for two young coppers. Any offers?'

'Right, sarge, on our way.'

As they passed him, tugging their clothes into shape and groping for the buttons that he'd curse at if they didn't get them done up fast, he muttered to himself, but loudly enough to thrum through the washroom: 'Bleedin' woodentops!'

A man was standing at the counter as they went through the outer office. 'Detective Inspector Galloway, please. The name's Langley. Harold Langley.'

He looked glum and tense. Lots of people who got drawn into Galloway's net looked glum. Better to be out on the streets, thought Carver: even when contaminated with rotten eggs – human or the other kind – there was fresher air in the streets than in the DI's troublesome mind and troublesome office.

'What's the chance of two in one day, d'you reckon?' he said blithely to Taffy Edwards.

'Oh, got the taste, have you?'

They fell companionably into step. Everything was set fair for a quiet hour or two, keeping the peace – most of all their own.

A transit van skidded to the kerb beside them. 'Come on, that team of dippers are at it again. Two WPCs hit the wire.' As they were scrambling into the back, the driver shouted over his shoulder: 'Might flush 'em out this time. High Street, one of the big stores. Hold on.' They swung sharp left, slowed, veered, and shot ahead.

Roy Galloway watched Bob Cryer approaching past the glass partition. He looked cheerful. Galloway gritted his teeth. If Cryer looked cheerful it often meant he had something up his sleeve.

'Roy, want some good news? PC Litten's just attended a break-and-enter. Sounds like the MO you're interested in. Scenes of Crime are on their way. I've told Litten to stay put and touch nothing.'

'That was bloody quick,' Galloway had to admit. 'Double-glazed, this drum?'

'The usual bloody mess inside. Bloody vandals. But no sign of entry. And according to Litten, yes, it's double-glazed.'

'That's my little firm.' The phone rang. Galloway answered it and felt his lips curl with pleasure; could almost feel himself getting his teeth into something at last. 'Spot on time. Just the right visitor. Three months of hard graft and it's paying off. Thanks, Bob.'

'Sometimes, Roy – only sometimes, mind – you can be quite human.'

'Get stuffed.'

The atmosphere was as normal. Healthy and normal.

Harold Langley was shown in. Galloway had had his questions pretty well lined up in advance. Now, with this latest news, he was ready to fire them all off at one hell of a rate. He didn't need to explain double glazing principles to Mr Langley, whose firm advertised its expertise in that field very widely in the area. Galloway knew the techniques and had piled up quite a few hunches about the men who worked on them. He could see from Langley's face that the boss of the firm was beginning to see what was coming: seeing it and fearing it.

'These fitters of yours,' said Galloway. 'Same team working on all your installations?'

'Small firm, inspector. Can't afford half a dozen different squads all over the place.'

'How long have these men worked for your company?'

'I'm not absolutely sure. You know how it is. I could get my people to check.'

'Roughly.'

Langley's dark, dour expression and the pout of his thick lips showed that he was more used to chatting up customers and overriding them with convincing patter than to answering hard, factual questions. 'Two years,' he ventured. 'Two and a half, give or take a few months.'

'Same routine, most days, most jobs? The fitters pick up their work sheets, I'd imagine, from your office – '

'Then go round to the factory and pick up the windows and doors required. They then go to the client's house and proceed with the installation. Straightforward.'

Galloway looked at his notepad and at a sketch he had had done by one of the lab boys on the last but three of successive break-ins. 'These doors. I presume they come complete?'

'Double-glazed doors in a hardwood frame.'

'Locks . . . keys?'

Langley looked worried but honest. 'Each door has a standard Yale-type lock and a mortice dead-bolt. Keys are taped to the doors to avoid getting mixed up.'

'So,' said Galloway, feeling it all click into place the way

21

one of those keys would click so neatly into place, 'it would be a simple task for dishonest fitters to have a spare pair of keys cut? Fit all the doors and windows, and then call back three months later, even six months later, and walk straight into the house?'

'I suppose it would.'

'And right at this moment, Mr Langley, it happens that we have another break-and-enter. Same pattern. Front door double-glazed, the lot. And it could just be your firm that fitted it. Think I'll have a car brought round so I can go and have a look. And those two fitters who do most of your work – on an installation right now, are they?'

It came out as a resigned whisper. 'I'll get on to my office for the address.'

'Do that, Mr Langley.'

He had no doubts about the conclusion. His only doubts were about PC Litten, when he got to the scene and had the lad fawning all over him. Litten was too big and brawny to fawn on anyone. But at least he had done everything he'd been ordered to do, and the fingerprint and photographic boys had got here in double-quick time. Hard not to give him an encouraging nod.

The thing was as good as wrapped up, there was no doubt about that. Galloway was in an expansive mood when he got back to Sun Hill. Sergeant Cryer was in much the same frame of mind. Quite a day, one way and another: their two main concerns both neatly wrapped up, with two double-glazing fitters being carted into custody, and two teams of dippers rounded up in one fell swoop. It was definitely a day for smiling.

Trust Bob Cryer to find a way of wiping the smile off anyone's face.

'You've got a visitor.'

'Sorry to be so popular, Bob.'

'Not the sort I'd want to be popular with, this one. Knew him way back. How Operation Countryman never dug him out of the dirt I'll never know.' Cryer puffed out an accusing breath and added sourly: 'One of *your* lot. A DS, name of Burnside.'

'Can't say I know him. What's he after, do you know?'

'At an educated guess I'd say he wants one of his snouts dropped out. Young Carver nicked a face earlier. We let him have one phone call, and he rang this Burnside. Shouting for a get-out, if you ask me. Only a guess, mind you. But it has that sort of stink about it.'

'Right, let's see the guy.'

As Galloway reached the foot of the stairs, Cryer said: 'He's too late, Roy. Mind you tell him that. The guy's nicked and charged.'

'That's what I like to see, Bob – co-operation.'

'Bloody superstars.'

Galloway stumped into his office. The man waiting for him was on his feet, with the sort of vague and guileless expression that made it clear he had been nosing through papers on the desk. He was a hulking six-footer with the jaw of a born bruiser, just as likely to have enjoyed being a criminal as being a police officer.

'Hello, sunshine, what can I do for you?'

'Burnside, guv. Hello. Well, guv, my guv'nor said I should pop over and speak to you. DI Hungerford. I think you know him.'

Yes, Roy Galloway knew Hungerford. But he wondered instinctively whether Hungerford had sent this Burnside character over here, or whether Burnside was in a spot and trying to get out of it under his own steam.

'Right. What's your problem?'

Burnside glanced meaningly at the chair facing the desk. Galloway waved him into it and sprawled back in his own chair. He didn't like the bloke's face or his manner.

'The thing is, guv, my best snout's gone and got himself lifted.'

'I just heard it might be that. So what?'

'Can you help, guv? You know how we need them. Specially when something's building up on our manor.'

Galloway knew all right. They all had to rely on greasy little villains to shop bigger villains. Never mind about the grease coming off on your own hands: there were times when a case simply could not be cracked unless you found the right little two-timer, the right snout.

'You're too late, son,' he said.

'He's done me some good in the past, and he's on to a big one for us right now. Real big number. You know how it is.'

'He's in the system. Already charged.'

'Oh, shit.' Burnside shook his head. 'My guv'nor won't be pleased, know what I mean?'

Galloway glared. 'A pox on your guv'nor. Don't you try that old number on me, toe rag.'

'Sorry, guv, I didn't mean . . . I mean, straight, I was only . . . look, guv, it's just that I need that body back out on the street. Need it bad. Was about due for a right result.'

Galloway tugged a lower desk drawer out with the toe of his shoe, and propped his foot on it. He stared at his foot rather than at Burnside. A nasty piece of work, almost as nasty as the people he was supposed to be fighting. But his story was likely enough, and the little rat downstairs wasn't going to be of any use tucked away in a cell.

'Yeah, well. I might just be able to swing that. But remember, the guy's still on to a nicking.'

'You can have him back in a few days, guv,' said Burnside eagerly. 'All I need is a few days.'

'I'll see what I can do.'

'And while you're at it, maybe I could have a few words with him?'

'See what I can do,' said Galloway again.

He hoisted himself to his feet. Burnside blundered up beside him, following him towards the door and down the stairs, trying to be matey, talking and rattling on. Galloway paid no attention.

Sergeant Cryer, at the foot of the stairs, watched them coming down. He wasn't offering them much in the way of a welcome.

Galloway said: 'Bob, could I have a word with you in my office?'

'I'll be . . .'

Cryer was interrupted by PC Hollis, hurrying through from the front office.

'Sarge, we've got a right pair at the desk. Fellow wants to log a citizen's arrest.'

'A what?'

'That's what he says. And there's a lot of blood about. I think we need the doctor.'

Cryer was on his way, calling back: 'Let me sort this out, Roy, and I'll be right with you.'

Three

Hollis had not exaggerated. There was indeed a fine old amount of blood around. The bigger man of the two was dripping it through the end of his shirt sleeve, torn and clutched to his fingers. Behind him, a dapper little man in his middle forties was still triumphantly twisting his captive's arm up behind his back.

'Dr Grimshaw's on the premises, sarge. Having a word with the super upstairs.'

'Thank God for that. Ask him to come down, will you?' Cryer urged the two men into the interview room and said: 'Please, sir, I think you can let the gentleman go now.'

'Not taking any chances, sergeant.'

'Please release your hold.'

Reluctantly the smaller man did so. The other stumbled ahead of him, crouching over the mess of his hand. Sergeant Cryer indicated two chairs. Behind him, Sergeant Penny came in, wondering what new freakishness the public were playing on them this time.

Cryer wondered the same.

'Now, sir . . . ?'

'My name is Skene, sergeant. Wilfred Skene. Simply doing my duty as a law-abiding citizen.'

'I'm sure, sir. Can you tell us exactly what happened?'

'This creature tried to pick my pocket. My inside pocket.' Skene sounded genuinely outraged, as if attempts on an inside pocket were ten times worse than a simple dip into an outer jacket pocket.

'And you made a citizen's arrest.' Cryer and Penny looked

disbelievingly at the bloodstained fingers and shred of what had once been a white shirt.

'That is so. His friends, I'm afraid, got away.'

'Not for long, I'm sure,' said Cryer reassuringly. He beamed at the slumped, shuddering man beside Skene. 'I bet that shocked you, eh? . . . *Fingers!*'

Skene, with mock diffidence, opened his jacket to display the inner pocket. Sewn along the lip of the pocket was a neat line of fish-hooks.

'An old trick I picked up whilst living in Hong Kong, sergeant.'

'That was quite a catch, sir.' Penny's comment combined admiration with uncertainty.

Cryer felt the same uncertainty. He was none too sure it was legal to go around fitted out like that, even to trap pickpockets. But what sort of charge could you bring? Possession of an offensive weapon . . . possession of an offensive pocket . . . ?

There was a tap at the door. Cryer, the nearest, opened it.

Dr Grimshaw said: 'I'm told you have a casualty for me.'

'That's right, doc. A man with injured fingers. Right in here.' As Grimshaw went on into the room, he added: 'By the way, how's the chap who had that fit? Pull round all right, did he?'

Grimshaw stopped, not looking round.

'Oh. Sorry, doc.' Cryer waved at Sergeant Penny. 'Can you take over and start the paperwork, Tom? Better go and see what Galloway's got in mind.'

He would have liked to say something consoling to Dr Grimshaw, but it wasn't his place to do so. And it wouldn't have done any good. A man had died. No use telling a doctor – least of all one usually as conscientious as Grimshaw – that you couldn't win 'em all, that we all made mistakes, that it was a rough old life and folk were dropping dead every second of the day.

It was going to haunt Grimshaw, that one error: he was that sort of man.

Cryer went upstairs and into Roy Galloway's office.

Galloway said: 'You told me porkies, Bob. You told me the snout had been processed and charged.'

'Well – '

'I just checked. He hasn't been charged, has he, my old son?'

'He will be as soon as we get the bit from CRO.'

'But he hasn't been charged yet,' said the detective inspector inexorably.

'All right, not yet. But I'm not dropping him out, Roy, no way.'

'Who said I wanted him dropped out?'

'Well, that's what Burnside's after, isn't it? Why else am I here?'

'All I'm asking for is – '

'He ain't walking, Roy, and that's it. He was caught fair and square. It's PC Carver's first collar, and you know what that means to a kid. And all that apart, you don't need telling my feelings about these silly games.'

'No, I don't need telling.' Galloway battered on: 'All I'm asking for is a couple of days. Don't charge him now. Bail him out to attend this station at a later date.'

'On what grounds?'

'In order that further inquiries be made regarding the property found in his possession. It can all be official. No problem.'

Cryer looked down his nose. There was a lot of it to be looked down. 'My, but you've got all the answers, ain't you, Roy?'

'I try, Bob. I try.'

Cryer turned and went out.

Galloway gave him time to get clear, then went down to see how Burnside was getting on with his pet squeaker. As he opened the door, Burnside was saying:

'You're a pain in the arse, Lennie. Caused me a right lot of aggravation. And you know what I can be like when I get naused.'

The cowering little thing on the other side of the table twitched his ferrety nose uncontrollably. 'I'm sorry, Mr Burnside, really. Straight up. I had to do a bit, I needed the poppy real bad. Had to have some, you know how it is.'

'You should have come to me, then, shouldn't you? You're rubbish, Lennie. Bleeding rubbish.'

His hand was raised, and Lennie was cringing, when they both became aware of Galloway in the doorway.

Burnside smirked. 'All right, guv?'

'You've got half a result, right? Just the way you suggested it. Understood?'

The snout looked questioningly from one to the other.

'What's that mean, Mr Burnside? Half a result. Look, I'm clear, ain't I? It's all right. You wouldn't let me down, not you, Mr Burnside.'

Burnside put a hand on his collar and lifted him to his feet. Galloway shrugged and turned away, leaving them to their happy reunion; but a few words drifted back along the echoing corridor as Burnside hustled Lennie away to the outside world.

'Just one thing, you. I gotta bring you back in about a week's time. Don't worry, no aggro. The guv'nor back there just wants to have a little chat, that's all.'

You're sure, Mr Burnside? Nuffing heavy?'

'Lennie, would I wet up your leg, son?'

The outer door above the car park swung shut behind the two of them.

In the distance Bob Cryer was calling: 'Carver? You up there? Just nip along to the parade room, will you?'

Jimmy Carver had taken more than his share of ribbing. What with Taffy going on and on about his speed – 'Wouldn't stand a chance of bringing him down at Cardiff Arms Park, not any of them, I'm telling you' – and Dave Litten asking how Carol at the café had taken it and what else was she hoping to get in the near future and then going into details about his own thoughts regarding Carol and that dress of hers and the bits not altogether covered by her dress, he was almost glad to be summoned by Sergeant Cryer.

'What you been up to, then?' Litten was in no mood to give up the joshing. 'Sounds like aggro.'

'Just a pat on the back,' said Taffy. 'Don't worry, Jimbo.'

'A pat on the back – from *him*?' Litten raised his gaze despairingly to the ceiling. 'You've got to be joking.'

Carver made his way to the parade room with no idea what to expect.

When the door had clicked shut, the sergeant looked past him, somehow avoiding his eyes. A vein pulsed in his neck. He looked angry, all tightened up. Carver wondered what on earth had gone wrong.

Cryer said: 'Just thought I'd bring you up to date, son. Wouldn't want you to hear it from anyone else. That was a nice collar you made today. Nobody's going to take that away from you. But just for the record, we're not charging him today.'

That made no sense. Carver stared. 'Not charging him, sarge?'

'You didn't listen, son.' Cryer was still taut and fuming, but not at Carver. 'I didn't say we're not charging him. I said we're not charging him today.'

'Why, sarge? Did I do something wrong? I did everything the way I thought – '

'No, son. You did all right.' Cryer let out a snort of disgust. 'Look, from time to time we have to play silly buggers. Bend the rules slightly. None of us like it but it has to be done when there's bigger fish to catch.'

'But he will *be* charged?' Carver persisted.

'Of course he will. He's . . . he's just being released pending further inquiries on the property found in his possession.'

'Released? But – '

'You heard, lad.'

Carver drew himself up and waited for Sergeant Cryer to leave the room. He paused, trying to keep his hands steady.

He wanted to lash out and take a poke at the wall, for all the good that would have done.

He went out into the corridor.

'All right, Jimbo?' Taffy came out of the shadow of the staircase. 'No problem?'

'No.'

You don't look very happy, boyo.'

'Forget it.'

'Come on, what's up?'

'Nothing. I've told you, forget it.'

They checked their buttons, tugged their tunics straight, and went to the main entrance.

A car turned out of the car park, gathering speed. Burnside was driving. Beside him, Lennie leaned out and jabbed two fingers derisively in the air as the car passed the two constables.

Behind Carver, Galloway said in a wry tone: 'Funny ol' business is cops and robbers, son. Very funny indeed.'

Four

There was often a fair old racket in the station canteen, and a good deal of leg-pulling. Today there was even more noise than usual, but no leg-pulling. Today things were deadly serious.

Tables had been pushed back against the wall out of the way, except for one behind which Chief Superintendent Brownlow sat, flanked by Detective Inspector Galloway. Brownlow's pouchy, bulldog features were heavy with the need for self-control as he faced the angry audience sitting on hastily assembled rows of chairs, or pushing themselves upright, shouting, arguing, talking over the deep, level voice of their own spokesman.

They were in no mood to listen. They had come here to make themselves heard and let their tempers run wild. You couldn't blame them for their anger. Clayview council estate looked new and smart enough, with its flats in well-organized blocks instead of high-rise monsters; the patches of green and a scattering of trees made it a desirable area, quite a credit to the local planners. But below its brightness there was dark menace. There were about two hundred youngsters living there – and out of that two hundred, thirty were known heroin addicts. Two had died of drugs overdoses: one found in a public lavatory, the other dumped at the hospital gates. There would be more to come. The men and women venting their rage on the two police officers were parents, scared out of their wits, wanting to take it all out on somebody.

'Let's have some action, instead of just sitting there like – '

'Never nick any of 'em unless they park on a double yellow line, will yer?'

'Quiet, please.' Tombo Robinson had been pushed forward to speak for them. A tall, handsome Trinidadian with a resonant voice, he was trying to keep things calm. 'You're not helping us. You're not helping me. But Mr Brownlow, Mr Galloway, you just gotta realize – '

'They're not going to do anything. You've only got to look at their faces.'

'They don't want to know.'

A woman with a taped-up pair of National Health glasses put her head out from behind Robinson's imposing bulk. 'You wanna come and see my lad. Sixteen, that's all, and just a bloody cabbage. That's all he frigging well is. Thanks to them drug peddlers. And no thanks to you layabouts for – '

'Do you want me to put our views forward in a proper manner, yes or no?' demanded Robinson.

'Take the law into our own hands, that's the only way.'

'String the bastards up . . .'

Brownlow put his hands on the table and pushed himself slowly to his feet. He was deliberately taking it calmly, playing it slow and heavy and unruffled. Galloway fidgeted. Never patient at the best of times, he wanted some plain talking, not low-temperature soothing stuff.

'We are as concerned as you are about the increase in heroin abuse,' said the chief superintendent. 'But let me say right away that you, as parents, also have a responsibility. A responsibility to speak out – '

'What the 'ell d'you suppose we've been doing?'

'To speak out and keep us informed, all the way along the line. Responsibility to others, as well. This war isn't restricted to your estate. It's a national epidemic. A world-wide one. We shall only succeed if – '

'It's our estate we're talking about, right here and now. Not bloody China.'

Brownlow took up a sheet of paper and read the figures out loud. Over the past three months there had been twenty-three arrests for possession of heroin, and sixteen for supplying. That success had been achieved as a direct result of

33

criminal intelligence, and interpretation of such information as had been put forward through the tenants' association. It wasn't a bad achievement. But they had to keep working away at it, all of them.

'But these users you keep nicking,' protested a man at the back of the room, 'they're our kids, that's who – not the pushers. Don't you understand what we're getting at?'

Robinson said earnestly: 'What we are saying to you, Mr Brownlow, is that we have done our best to furnish you with names and addresses, but these same people are still walking the estate. Still supplying drugs!'

'Simply because the heroin found in their possession is of a small quantity, never enough to back up the charge of large-scale supplying. That weakens the evidence submitted in court.'

'You just let 'em slip through your fingers. You don't bloody care.'

Roy Galloway could hold back no longer. When he rose to his feet it was not slowly and portentously. He got up fast, and kicked his chair back.

'I'm sorry, but I've listened to this long enough. You've been carrying on plenty about us not doing our job, not nicking the pushers. But it's *your kids*! Face up to it, that's what we're talking about. Most of your own kids are doing the pushing, financing their own addiction. We can run 'em in all right – and you'll be the first to scream blue bloody murder. The people we need are the big ones, the scum who are supplying those kids.' He slammed his fist down on the table. 'I'll bet some of you sitting there even know who the real dealers are.'

'Now wait a minute – '

'You know where that heroin's coming from, and I still say a couple of you, maybe more, have an idea who the dealers are. Perhaps you're too frightened to say. All *I* can say is we'll get nowhere if you're too scared to speak out. Get together. Confide in each other. Let us know, then we can really do something about this problem. Only don't leave it too late, because every hour that goes by, another kid gets hooked. You know what I'm talking about?'

There was a silence. The parents viewed him with wary respect.

Brownlow cleared his throat. 'Yes, well . . . I think perhaps this is an opportune moment to break for tea and biscuits.'

While the tenants queued up by the urn and munched biscuits, some still arguing with their mouths full, the two officers and Tombo Robinson drew away into a corner.

'I'm sorry if they got unruly at times,' said Robinson, 'but it's understandable, Mr Brownlow. They're worried parents. Very worried.'

'It's a pity we couldn't all have got together earlier. Now we've started, we've got to follow it up. As Inspector Galloway said, every hour that goes by, somewhere another youngster will be introduced to heroin.'

'I think you made that point. Oh, yes. And I think we'll be giving you the names of some pushers. Bit by bit, you understand? Where they live, where they hang out.' Robinson glanced cautiously at Galloway. 'They may not be the top people, but we have to start somewhere. You know, if there's any more I can do you've only got to ask.'

It was the chance Galloway had been waiting for. He was not going to risk consulting Brownlow. With sudden forcefulness, his finger prodding threateningly, he said: 'Listen, Tombo. You and I have a pretty good idea where the pushers get their "smack" from. Stop giving us the run-around. If you're scared, say so. But if you're not, let's be hearing from you.'

'If I knew, don't you think I'd be telling you?'

Brownlow turned his back on the rest of the room, keeping his voice down but putting some weight behind it. 'Please, gentlemen, not too much noise. And you're out of order, Inspector Galloway.'

'Out of order, am I? Well, let me tell you, sir, with respect . . . I'm the only one who seems to know what's going on,

35

on this manor. All right! You want me to tell you where the heroin's coming from? Decker's Club. How about that?'

'Decker's?' said Robinson sceptically.

'The old cinema?' Brownlow was equally unimpressed. 'You've never mentioned that before, Roy. I know it was an illegal drinking club way back, but we put an end to that. Raided it so many times they packed up and disappeared.'

'Well, they've started up again. Nice and quiet and respectable. Only this time they're into drugs.'

'Decker's?' said Robinson again. 'Harry Decker back in town? I can't believe it.'

'You'd better, my old son, because that's where the action is.'

'If it's true,' fretted Brownlow, 'we'll have one hell of a job getting in there. The place is like a maze. Some of those raids we tried in the past were disastrous.'

'Not if we had an inside man.'

The two of them exchanged glances and then turned to stare at Robinson.

He took a step back. 'Oh, no! I haven't been mixed up with that firm for years.'

'You'd be just the man,' said Galloway.

'You can't ask me. I've got a family. They'd cut my throat!'

'I understand, Mr Robinson,' Brownlow soothed him. 'Inspector Galloway shouldn't have asked you.'

'You were once a member,' said Galloway remorselessly. 'You're the ideal man.'

'I don't mix with those people any more. Don't mix with those kind of people. Don't you understand?'

'Look, Tombo. If you want to stop those people poisoning your kids, then you get me and my men into Decker's and this time we'll cut off the supply. It'll give us the chance we need. Come on, what d'you say?'

Robinson took a deep breath. In the background the others began to clatter their teacups noisily back on to the table as a signal that they were ready to get back to the argument.

Robinson muttered: 'Nobody to know except you and Mr Brownlow?'

'Got yourself a deal, Tombo.'

The chief superintendent's office was quieter than the canteen. On the other hand, Brownlow was looking more fierce than he had allowed himself to be in front of their visitors.

'You shouldn't have done it, Roy. I can see all kinds of complications. What if he gets sussed out, beaten up – or even worse? You put me in an awkward position, Roy.'

Galloway said nothing.

'And Decker's of all places!' Brownlow exploded. 'Why in hell didn't you come to me in the first place? Give *me* the information? It makes me look as if I don't know what's going on in my own division.' He dragged open a drawer, took out a bottle of whisky and two glasses, poured drinks and handed one to the detective inspector, with the air of one offering a draught of poison rather than a sociable drink. 'How long have you held back this information, Roy?'

Galloway took a warming gulp before risking the answer. 'I haven't.'

'What do you mean, you haven't?'

'It's . . . well, an educated guess, that's all.'

'Am I hearing right?'

'Only heard today that Decker's had been started up again.' Galloway tried to keep it airy and light-hearted. 'Illegal drinking, ponces, pimps, that kind of thing. Up to their old games. Only I bet you find this recent increase in heroin started about the same time Decker's turned up on the manor again. As I said, it's an educated guess.'

'And you've put in an inexperienced undercover man – an amateur, one of the great general public – on an educated guess?'

'Tombo will be all right. Once he's eased himself into Decker's, he'll come up with something. I know him. He'll find *something*.'

'I don't like it. When will he get in touch?'

'When he's got something to show. It'll take time. He can't just walk in there and wrap it all up in twenty-four hours. He'll ring me, we'll meet. We'll play it clever.'

'You'd better. I hope for your sake this doesn't go wrong, Roy.' Brownlow emptied his glass and began riffling through papers on his desk. 'Now, while you're here, there's something else.'

In this job there was always something else. Galloway sighed. 'Yes, guv?'

'Statistics.' Brownlow selected one sheet of paper and flapped it in the air. 'Statistics and more statistics.'

'Not quite my line, guv.'

'Trouble is it has to be everybody's line nowadays. All for the benefit of the Home Office. Now, these . . . um . . . bomb hoaxes.'

Galloway snorted. 'Those phone calls to restaurants? Been hearing about them, yes. All pranks, if you ask me.'

'The trouble is that when the Home Office match up our statistics with others in the Met, they're coming up with a different story.'

'There've only been three on our patch. Surely that doesn't constitute a problem?'

'Two of those were Jewish restaurants.'

'Perhaps somebody doesn't like salt beef.'

Brownlow scowled. 'Not what I call a very constructive remark. Let me tell you, Roy, the Home Office is breathing down the Commissioner's neck, and I'm getting some of the draught.'

Galloway restrained himself from making a further snide remark. It was really too crazy. Racial hoaxes? Arabs . . . terrorists? He said: 'This is just stupid pranks.'

'I won't beat about the bush. I want you to take over the investigation. And wrap it up fast.'

'Now, hang on, sir. I mean, Sergeant Cryer's dealing with that. I don't think I should interfere.'

'I've got the greatest respect for Sergeant Cryer, but his work load's been heavy over the last two weeks. On top of that he's got another graduate attached to him: PC Higgins. Unfortunately I don't have any other sergeants with his experience free at the moment.'

Galloway said levelly: 'You mean, on top of the heroin hurry-up I've got to work miracles on the restaurant lark as well, all overnight?'

'You've said yourself that it'll take a little while for Robinson to ease himself into that place. While you're waiting, you can tackle this one. If you're right and it's a prank, then I want it cleared up and out of the way. Just liaise with Sergeant Cryer, get the details from him, and take over.' Before Galloway could raise any further objections, the chief superintendent said: 'Good. Thank you, Roy.'

'Thank you, sir.' When well away from the room, Galloway said it louder: 'Thank you *very* much.'

'Hello, guv.' PC Litten grinned obsequiously. 'Keeping you busy, are they?'

Galloway brushed past him and clattered halfway down the stairs. 'Sergeant Cryer! I want to see you in my office. *Now!*'

Cryer kept him waiting. Deliberately: Galloway could be sure of that. He was in a mood to punch a fist into that beak when it finally came round the door.

'This is a bloody lumber, this one!'

Cryer stared. 'Got something on our mind, have we?'

'At least one of us has *got* a mind. Having to sort out the messes you lot get yourselves into.'

'Such as?'

'Such as this codswallop about restaurants and phone calls. Letting it drift on until I get lumbered with it. So. Just give me any details you've managed to trip over these last few weeks, and let me show you how to settle it. Fast.'

'Look,' said Bob Cryer, 'this isn't one of those jobs you can go into crash, bang, wallop. You have to sniff around. Use a bit of tact. But you wouldn't know what that means, would you?'

'I know what action means, and there's going to be some.

39

Tact? Who've you been tactful with – and how far has it got you? Bloody idleness, more like.'

'You haven't got Solly Goldstein and Reggie Abrahams shouting at you from one side, and the chief super from the other.'

'But it's a prank,' yelled Galloway. 'Can't you see that?' His voice drew attentive glances from the next office. He got up and slammed the door. 'Look, I know Solly Goldstein. Believe me, if there was no PLO, he'd have invented it.'

'You do talk some bloody rubbish sometimes, you honestly do. You can't treat calls like that as a joke, you have to go through the procedures as if it was the real thing. Every time you have to treat it for real. There's no short cuts.'

'After three phone calls there must be some MO to follow up. *Something*!' Galloway waved at the door. 'All right, leave it with me. The CID will sort it all out, as per usual.'

Cryer paused at the door. 'One of these days, Roy Galloway, you're going to come tumbling off that high horse of yours, and no one's going to lift a finger – least of all me.'

'Forget the violins, Robert. Tell you what' – Galloway took a ten-pound note from his wallet and slammed it on the desk – 'there you are, that says I'll crack it.'

Cryer stared down at the note. 'Two weeks?'

Galloway nudged the note an inch towards him. Cryer took out a tenner of his own and slapped it down to cover the other.

'Two weeks,' said Galloway, 'at the outside.'

Five

Maureen Galloway said: 'Don't answer it!'

The phone had begun to ring just as they came back into the house. They had been down the road for an Indian. It always had quite an effect on Maureen: something about a really first-rate Tandoori tickled her appetite – more than one of her appetites. She had been nuzzling her cheek against her husband's as they came up the path, and even without the food he would have got that same warm, glowing sensation inside.

But the phone was ringing.

'You're off duty,' she said. 'Let it ring.'

He put out a hand towards the hall table. She tugged away from him, then tried to catch his arm.

He said: 'It might be – '

'Whoever it might be, are they all that more important than me?'

Any second now the noise would stop. Galloway snatched up the receiver.

'Penny here, inspector. We've got another bomb hoax. I thought you'd want to know.'

'Where?'

'Dimitri's Greek and Continental nosh house. You know it?'

'I know it.'

'The area car's already round there with your Sergeant Roach. He thought you'd want to – '

'I'll be right with 'em.'

He turned to explain to Maureen and promise that he would be back in half an hour – well, no more than an hour anyway – but she was already storming up the stairs and giving him a look over the banisters which was not what you'd call inviting.

No sense of priorities, women.

Galloway knew all the back doubles and was at Dimitri's door within fifteen minutes. A 'Closed' sign dangled in the glass panel, but the door was open and at any rate one person was managing to snatch a quick snack: Sergeant Roach swallowed down a hasty mouthful and tried to look alert and dutiful as he scrambled to his feet.

'Inspector Galloway, my friend.' Dimitri's smile was wide, his arms were spread wide, he was offering the whole place on a plate – or in a glass. 'You would like a drink?' Without waiting for an answer he gestured to the man leaning behind the bar, and a triple-sized ouzo was set on the edge of the counter.

'Right. What's the form?'

It was the same pattern, just the same as the others. There had been a phone call to say that a bomb on the premises was due to go off any minute. Then the caller rang off, and customers were hustled out without more ado. Dimitri had called the police in right away, and the premises had been thoroughly cleared and searched. Then they were gone over again with a fine tooth-comb, taking no chances. If there had been a suspect package, the experts would have come in and padded round it very soft-shoe, breathing in that silent way they had.

There was nothing.

'I knew it was a hoax as soon as the man spoke,' said Dimitri. 'But you take no chances, no? I have to hurry everybody out. Only now I want to know. I want you to find out.'

'Right, Ted.' Galloway nodded at Roach, who was looking wistfully at a few shreds of kebab cooling on his abandoned plate. 'You and Mike call it a day. Take those uniformed bods down in the van with you, and I'll see you in the morning. Right?'

'You want me to put anything in the book?'

'I'll do it myself. Dimitri and I are going to go over everything, aren't we, Dimitri? Every little detail. Even if it takes all night.'

It had not occurred to him that such a corny phrase could come so close to the truth. He and Dimitri sat down, and ouzo was poured; and then, within surprisingly few minutes, more ouzo was poured. It did not appear to slow down Dimitri's explanations of what had happened, but after a while it began to slow down Galloway's comprehension.

Maybe, he thought muzzily, not a bad thing. In a sort of trance he began to reach for wisps of truth through a haze of speculation.

There were things in Dimitri's head which the volatile Cypriot did not even know he had absorbed. He talked about the phone call, talked about the rumours he had heard about bombs – hoaxes and the real thing – and tried several imitations of the caller's voice, all of them unconvincing and no two even resembling each other. It was quite some time, well into the fifth or sixth ouzo and the third dish of black olives, that he said something which penetrated Galloway's drowsy but dogged mind.

'Well,' he said plaintively after Galloway had sneered for the third time at his grotesque impersonations, 'it was not so easy, you know? I am supposed to pick up an accent with all that noise going on?'

'Shouldn't have so much noise in a high-class eaterie like this.'

'Not here. Behind this man, the one who talks to me. Roadworks.'

'Roadworks?'

'Behind him, you hear it, the drill, things going over a sheet of metal or something. You know how it is.'

'Roadworks?' Galloway repeated. 'On Friday night?'

Dimitri looked doubtful, then confident. 'Sound of a drill,' he said. 'Cars over a loose piece of sheet metal. I hear it just like that, you understand?'

'Can I use your phone?'

Dimitri waved a lordly hand.

Galloway rang first Solly Goldstein and then Reggie Abrahams. It was made clear to him that he had not chosen the most tactful time. The Jewish Sabbath was already under way, and Solly and Reggie were not best pleased to be interrupted with squalid weekday affairs at such an hour. But they were charitable men, and they told Galloway what he wanted to know. It was indeed what he wanted to know. They remembered, when nudged, that noise in the background, just the way Dimitri had said. Which narrowed it down. Somewhere on the patch, roadworks which went on through the evening – even a Friday evening.

Galloway felt pleased with himself. Lurching back from the phone, the waywardness of his lower limbs made him less pleased. But another ouzo from Dimitri restored the balance, even if only temporarily.

He went home with a great sensation of righteousness swilling around inside. It made quite a cocktail, added to the ouzo.

Home was not all that homely. The bed was empty. He swayed over it, swayed backwards, put a hand on the bedside lamp to stop it wobbling, and made a mental resolve to tell Maureen to get it fixed before it blew up, or fell apart, or did whatever else was in its evil mind.

Only where the hell was Maureen?

He contemplated the space from which two pillows had been removed, and considered going to the spare room to ask if she had a headache, or a bad cold, or something.

Then he decided against it.

He made an excursion to the bathroom, and did not much care for the results. He ought to have known better. As an acquaintance of Dimitri's all this time, he certainly ought to have known better. The trouble was, the ouzo had tasted so much smoother and friendlier then than it tasted now.

It was on his third visit to the bathroom, at some hour of the morning to which he would never have wished to testify in court, that things began to swim back into focus. Way down there in his subconscious was something that must have been nagging at him from earlier in the evening; or the night; or whenever.

A prank, he had told Brownlow. And Bob Cryer. And a prank it was.

Human nature, that's what it was: that old plague of all good policemen, plain-clothes or otherwise. Just look at it. If you were in a restaurant and the place was cleared because of a bomb threat, and you hadn't paid your bill, what would you do? Honest blokes would go back next day, or put a cheque in the post, or at the very least fork out next time they went in. Particularly if the restaurant knew them.

Which of course was the point.

Galloway ran his tongue round his mouth and wondered why he was so irresistibly reminded of the bottom of a parrot's cage, when he hadn't been on speaking terms with a parrot since his grandmother's had been eaten by next door's tabby cat.

This had to be it. You narrowed down the field, and the pattern began to emerge. Right in the middle of that field, a right couple of scarecrows, were these two fellows. Solly hadn't said it in so many words, and Reggie Abrahams hadn't been sure enough to point the finger: but there were two shapes in there, and in Dimitri's place. Just suppose two jokers in each restaurant each time there was one of those bomb calls, and just suppose the calls came just when the bill had been presented: a bill that was never paid. And then there had to be the third party, the person who made the call . . .

From the same phone box.

Galloway crashed back into bed. There was not much to be done about it until Monday morning; but tomorrow, Sunday (or was it sliding well into Sunday already?), Ted Roach could get out on the manor and start asking around about two likely lads, and notifying restaurants, and jumping up and down on sheets of metal near telephone boxes if necessary.

He slept.

When he awoke, there were noises downstairs. Even from a distance they gave him a headache – or, rather, increased the pressure on the iron band round his forehead. Also there was a smell of bacon frying. It usually enticed him out of bed and down the stairs in a fine, hearty, greedy mood.

This morning he went yet again to the bathroom.

She was cruel. She must have known what she was doing. He was surprised she hadn't put garlic and onions with it, and set fire to the toast just to add to the general aroma.

He made a stab at getting dressed, and was tolerably proud of the results, even if he did have to put dark glasses on before picking up his pink striped shirt. There was no way, however, that he could get his cufflinks into the right holes. Each time he prodded the shank through one hole he either cut himself on the sharper link or got his thumb snarled up with a stray thread.

Finally he went downstairs and tried to kiss Maureen. He missed, and narrowly escaped falling across the kitchen table.

He held out his right arm, with the cufflink dangling. 'Could you . . . ?'

'It serves you right,' she said very quietly.

The bacon spat in the pan.

'Coffee?' he ventured.

'I fancy China tea right now.'

Heroin dealers weren't going to beat Roy Galloway. Shady little pranksters in restaurants weren't going to beat him. Nor was Bob Cryer. But there were times when he had to admit defeat. He left home without attempting that happy peck on the cheek which had become standard practice, and found his way to Sun Hill nick, where WPC Ackland smiled at him and then went pale, Ted Roach said, 'How did it go, guv?' and then decided not to pursue the matter, and young Dashwood showed his worthiness for promotion by scurrying about in search of black coffee and a supply of aspirins.

'Roadworks,' said Galloway when he had got his voice under some sort of control. 'On overtime. And a trench or a gap, or something, with a sheet of metal across it. Start looking.'

That was enough for starters. He groped for another helping of aspirin.

Six

Saturday turmoil in the streets was pretty much the same as any other day, but with some different faces, some faces missing, and not quite the same tempo. Jimmy Carver was getting used to the shifts and changes and differences of emphasis.

A lot of the riverside warehouses worked on Saturdays, but there were fewer delivery lorries and a lot more punters driving more slowly in their cars, looking for wine bargains or for snips in the street market.

He glanced sideways at PC Higgins to see what impact it was all making. Not much, from the look on Higgins's pale and rather disdainful face.

Sergeant Cryer had sounded a bit dubious earlier this morning before the two of them set out.

'I don't usually let new boys out with such inexperienced officers as Carver here. On the other hand, he hasn't learnt all of the bad habits yet, not like some of the reprobates you've been out with this week, Higgins.'

Was WPC Ackland smiling at Jimmy Carver, or snickering at him?

'Keep out of trouble,' said Cryer in that tone they were so used to that they could almost turn the volume right down and still get the message good and clear. 'And remember, anything you can't handle, straight on the blower.'

Carver sympathized with Higgins; or tried to. It seemed only yesterday that he himself had been thrown in at the deep end, just like this. They ought to have something in common. But Higgins was holding his head proudly back and staring ahead like some explorer who had just seen the promised land and was not much concerned with trivial things under his own nose. Not a matey sort, Higgins. Either he would go far or he'd get nowhere at all.

Carver said tentatively: 'What d'you make of it so far, then?'

'I expected to get more practical experience.' Higgins gave a contemptuous glance at three young yobbos mimicking his walk and the way he swung his arms. 'I thought I'd learn more this week in that respect, but nobody seems particularly keen to take me out, show me anything. I'm treated with suspicion.'

That, at any rate, Carver could remember. Of course they took their time sizing you up. You might have thought your probationary period was technically over, but there was still a trial period to be gone through with the other lads. He tried to explain: 'It's not because anybody's got anything personal against you, Higgins – '

'Derek.'

'Mm?'

'I've told everybody my name's Derek. But nobody wants to know.'

'Look, I went through all that, just the same way, in my first few weeks. All the lads who've been here any length of time, they've got places to go – you know, cups of tea here, cups of tea there, and all that. I mean, they don't want you knowing about their perks.'

'I wouldn't tell.'

'Ah, but you might just come back as a senior officer. Then where would they be, eh?'

Derek Higgins preened himself and looked away with a flutter of mock modesty. Oh, Higgins knew all right where he intended to go.

Then his wandering gaze settled. 'What's that?'

They stopped by a doorway into what on weekdays was a grotty arcade leading to seedy offices behind the blacked-out windows of what had once been equally seedy shops. On a Saturday there was nothing much doing in there: except that today a huddled shape was stacked against the wall some way in from the street.

Carver led the way. It looked as if they had come across a stray from a wedding or a football match. But at this time of a Saturday morning . . . ?

They stooped over the crumpled figure. The smell that wafted up was a mixture of whisky and damp: not whisky and water, just booze and damp. He must have been there quite some hours.

'Right. Come on up, sir. You all right?'

The feeble answering moan released another sickly stench into the atmosphere.

'He's light as a feather,' marvelled Higgins. 'All skin and bone.'

'Come on. Wheel him along the road.' Carver made himself sound brisk and authoritative.

Higgins obeyed, obviously no more impressed by this experience than by any of the other routine jobs he had so far encountered.

Sergeant Cryer looked far from overjoyed. His immediate, instinctive wince made it clear that this was no new phenomenon, and the tottering, wheezing creature was no stranger to him.

'Lampton! Legless Lampton himself.'

'Ah, my dear old trusted friend.' The drunk tried to hold out his hand, but swayed perilously and had to be steadied by Higgins. 'Always said so, always will.'

'Higgins. Carver. Witness the act. Flannel from an expert. File him away in your mind so you'll be ready for him next time. Freelance journalist, one-time Fleet Street, and it's no wonder it's one-time and not any longer.' When Lampton said nothing, Cryer went on bitterly: 'Come on, let's have the latest. Don't disappoint my lads.'

'Sergeant, do I really have to go to court over this? Couldn't you show just a little ben . . . bl . . . benevolence? A caution, maybe?'

Carver looked away, and saw that Higgins was doing the

same. It was cruel to put this twitching wreck through this kind of thing.

But Cryer was inexorable. 'Cautions are over as far as you're concerned. Look, last week you nearly caused a bloody accident in the High Street. A few days before that, if it hadn't been for that special constable, you'd have been in the canal. So it's up before the beak on Monday morning, without fail. Carver!'

'Sarge?'

'Take him down to the pokey. When he sobers up, bail him.'

'A call, perhaps, at midday, officer? I'll be as right as rain then. And I'll promise, Scout's honour' – Lampton ventured an endearing grin – 'to be a good chap for the rest of the week.'

'I've heard your promises before. Go on, take him down.'

Carver and Higgins went through the ritual and were back on the street in ten minutes. It was an uneventful morning. Higgins complained again about the uselessness of it all. This wasn't going to do anything for his career. He had expected real action, expected to be plunged into real tough police work right away on a real tough manor, so he could distinguish himself, make his mark. Jimmy Carver nodded sagely with all the wisdom of several weeks on the beat behind him. Trouble was not something you needed to invite. It would come soon enough when it was good and ready, and Higgins might not like it when it did.

They returned to the station just as Lampton was making his way out of the side door. He clutched a brown paper bag to him, with a nearly empty whisky bottle in it. He was sober, but not looking as if he was enjoying it.

Carver squeezed back against the wall to let him pass. 'How are you feeling, sir?'

Lampton peered at them. 'You have me at a disadvantage, officer. Do we know each other?'

'Carver, sir. Higgins. We arrested you. Brought you in this morning.'

51

'So you did, yes. Thoughtful of you,' said Lampton sadly.

'You all right now, sir?'

'It's purely self-inflicted, young man. As your worthy sergeant so aptly puts it, it serves me bloody well right.'

Lampton went gingerly down the ramp. Higgins looked more and more disillusioned.

Jimmy Carver went on into the station and put his head round the door of the inner office. Taffy Edwards was sorting his way despairingly through a sheaf of crime sheets and making entries in his cramped handwriting. He hardly looked round when Carver spoke. No, he couldn't come for a drink right now. Yes, he knew there was only five minutes to go, but that wasn't the way Sergeant Cryer looked on it, and DI Galloway had been breathing down Cryer's neck just to make matters worse.

'Can I give you a hand?' Carver ventured.

'Yeah. Draw a firearm, put one up the spout, and just sort of wander into Galloway's office.'

'Well now, isn't that against the disciplinary code, PC Edwards?'

'What, shooting DIs?'

'No, drawing a firearm for private use.'

Taffy made a quick calculation. 'Look, Jim, I'll be about fifteen minutes. You go up the pub and I'll meet you there.'

Carver and Higgins changed and sauntered out into the street. It was a warm, sunny day. Carver drew a deep, appreciative breath and unzipped his black leather jacket, letting it swing loose. Great to think of Saturday afternoon all free and bright and sunny ahead.

He stopped by the door of the corner pub.

'Coming in for a quick one?'

Higgins looked uncomfortable. 'No, I don't think so. Got one or two things to do. I'll see you in the morning.'

Carver pushed the swing door and went in. A babble of voices seethed around him. Everybody else was feeling cheerful about Saturday, by the look of it. He fought his way to the counter.

'Two pints when you're ready, love.'

Sadie waved a buxom arm, uncapped three bottles of brown ale with three dexterous flicks of the wrist, and in minutes was heading towards him with two brimming, freshly pulled pints.

'Paid for,' she said.

'Oh, cheers, Sadie.'

'Not me, darling. The pain over there.'

Someone was writhing his way through the crowd. A flushed face came close to Carver's.

'My friend,' said Lampton. 'For a moment I thought I'd lost you.'

'Look, don't you think you've had enough of that stuff, Mr Lampton?' He watched the man sink a large whisky at one gulp and begin shoving the glass across the bar. 'I mean, I wouldn't like to see you being taken in again.'

'That stuff, as you so crudely put it, my friend, is inspiration. Ah, if only there were a reconciliation between my inspiration and my wayward pen!'

Taffy Edwards appeared at Carver's elbow and reached appreciatively for the full pint.

'Lovely. Cheers, Jim.'

'It was Mr Lampton bought you the drink, Taff.'

Edwards stared dubiously over the edge of his glass. In an undertone he said: 'That's not the drunk you nicked, is it?'

'Well, I – '

'Come on, Jim, time to go.'

'You've hardly started your drink yet, Taff.'

'Time to have it on your toes,' said Edwards loudly.

'While you two are arguing,' said Lampton, 'I'll just go and water the little feller.'

The moment he had lurched through the door at the end of the bar Edwards burst out: 'For God's sake, don't you know when to cut and run? It's a disciplinary offence to be associated with a man on bail, let alone bloody drink with him.'

'We can't just leave him like that.'

Sadie was edging her way through the crush, wiping sweat

from her brow, gathering up empty glasses. 'Look, your friend's had enough. I want him out. I can't afford to lose my licence. Just get him out.'

'He's coming back,' said Edwards. 'I'm off. Don't catch me sticking my neck out for any old drunk.'

He had gone by the time Lampton staggered lovingly back to Carver's side. 'One for the road?'

'I think I'd better see you along that road right now, sir.'

'But I don't want to –'

'Just tell me where you live, and I'll see you get there.'

In spite of mumbled protests he succeeded in steering Lampton to the door. Sadie watched them go with a nod of relief.

They had got themselves organized, just the way it had been before with the chop house, and then the two Jewish places, and then the Greek one. Tasty bit of nosh, that Greek gear, though really they both preferred pie and mash down the market. But when you could get it all for free, and take the mickey and get away with it . . . well, it was good for a giggle, and somehow the food tasted better when you knew you weren't going to have to pay for it.

Tonight they were going to be down the disco with a couple of birds who'd expect to have money spent on them. So the food today was going to be early afternoon: save spending too much tonight. Hungry for something else tonight.

Matty and Frankie had it all worked out. They had given young Kevin Lee at the paper stall the number of the restaurant, Chinese this time just to make a change. He knew the routine by now: knew how long to give them, when to nip round to the telephone box, and what to say. Actually they were doing him a favour: he got one hell of a kick out of it.

It had worked without a hitch so far. It was going to work again. Chop suey and special fried rice, some chicken, and then the phone call, panic, and away through the doors. It couldn't fail.

It was a giggle, that's all it was.

'About half past two, right?'

'Whatever you say.' Kevin had been delighted.

'And mind what *you* say. Same as before and nothing else, and don't hang about.'

'"There's a bomb in the gaff,"' Kevin recited, '"and it's goin' to go off any minute."'

'Good lad.'

The restaurant was up a narrow flight of stairs to the first floor, above a cycle shop and not too far from the street corner. Frankie made a quick assessment of the distance and the best direction. Wouldn't do to get held up by traffic near the junction. Then he sized up the staircase as they climbed to the first floor, noting which way the doors at top and bottom opened. No time to lose when the big bang threatened.

They had managed, the last couple of times, to get a table near the door, but here there were only two tables free, both of them in the middle of the room. They settled behind two large plastic-bound menus and covertly gauged the distance from here between other customers and the door, which opened inwards.

Right. No problem.

They ordered.

The service was quick and efficient. Too quick for comfort, really. To fill in time they had to order another couple of helpings – sweet and sour prawn balls, which dissolved like fluff in your mouth – and still there was a quarter of an hour to go before Kev set off the alarm.

Frankie gulped. He didn't go for the expression of that grave, dignified old fellow behind the little bar. Too much like some sinister mandarin out of a horror video.

'What'll you have?' asked Matty.

'I couldn't sink another thing, honest.'

'We can't hang about like a couple of prats, can we? We'd soon get sussed out.'

'I think the old geezer's already got his slant eyes on us.'

They tried to look away and pretend an interest in a silk picture of a placid riverside scene with a pagoda and bridge reflected in the water. It was a soothing picture; but they were not soothed.

Desperately Frankie ordered two coffees. The gaze of the proprietor behind the bar did not waver. The coffee was gone just as the clock behind his head showed half past two.

The phone did not ring.

Matty and Frankie watched the minute hand of the clock edge its way on. Still there was no sound.

Supposing the telephone box was being used, and Kevin couldn't get in? Or supposing it had been vandalized and he was dashing about looking for somewhere else?

'He's not going to ring,' breathed Matty. 'Better get some money out, see if we can pay up, and then get out of here.'

Frankie was stubborn. 'He's never let us down before.'

'We've got to do a runner.'

The phone rang. Frankie gasped and stared down, tense, into the dregs of his coffee. They were both poised, ready to move.

The man at the bar lifted the receiver; listened; stared straight at the two boys; then nodded to one of the waiters.

Frankie and Matty did not find out until later – much too late – that Kevin had been interrupted making the call from the local newsagent's, and had left the card with the phone number of the restaurant on it. But they knew, as one waiter positioned himself across the doorway to the toilets and another leaned back against the door to the stairs, that things were not going according to plan.

'Something's wrong,' said Matty. 'They've sussed us.'

'No. That must have been Kevin ringing. They don't know what to do, that's what it is. Give 'em time to sort themselves out.'

56

'They ain't going to empty the place. You can see that. You can see we're going to be grabbed.'

'Not if I can help it, we ain't.' Frankie shoved himself up on his feet and shouted across the room: 'Quick, there's a bomb! It'll go off any minute. Get moving, everybody out now! *Now!*'

There was a moment's pause, as if nobody had taken it in, or maybe nobody thought it was anything but a joke. Then it registered. A woman screamed, and began groping her way towards the door. The waiter there shook his head and refused to step out of the way. Two men from a table in the window shouted and ran to join her, pushing the waiter bodily aside.

At the same moment the door from the kitchen swung open. Two men erupted, brandishing huge kitchen knives. For a hysterical second Frankie wanted wildly to make a joke about not knowing you needed such large choppers to carve up bean sprouts. But then someone crashed across their path, a man's arm went up to protect himself, and there was a spurt of blood and a shout of agony. Then the two Chinese hit the two boys, and there was nothing to joke about.

Jimmy Carver heard the screaming as he steered Lampton warily round the street corner. He had been taking it easy, with half of his mind contemplating the free afternoon ahead. Other feet could plod this beat until tomorrow morning. Even so, it was impossible not to notice things from the corner of your eye. Once a copper, always a copper, even when you were off duty. You didn't walk along a street like anybody else, minding your own business and thinking your own thoughts while the world went by: instinctively you noticed a kid acting the fool on a bike – doing wheelies in the middle of the pavement with all those young mothers and their prams about! – and two men muttering in a doorway with their heads averted . . . hatching what bit of aggro? Not to mention playing guardian angel to this pathetic, drunken git.

Carver tried to quicken the pace once they were round the

corner. Then came the screaming, above the rumble of traffic and the pounding of rock music from a record store. People were shoving and shouting and falling across the pavement right ahead.

'A bomb!'

'It's a hoax. They said it – '

'Oh, God, look at *him*.'

A man was collapsed at the foot of the Chinese restaurant stairs. Blood was gouting from his arm, over the shallow step and down on to the pavement.

Carver wrenched himself away from Lampton, leaving him to totter forward under his own steam. He elbowed his way through the crowd, dragging his jacket off.

'Put this under his head. *You* – phone an ambulance.'

The snap of command in his tone cut through any protest the bystander might have felt like making. He was on his way to the phone box as the welcome shapes of two uniformed officers hove into view – a PC and a WPC, both of them known to Carver but never appreciated as much as now. Messages went out; and from Sun Hill police station they came reassuringly back.

In a matter of minutes the ambulance rolled up. Plus another one for the mincemeat which the Chinese kitchen staff had made of the two moaning, shivering brothers.

And Detective Inspector Galloway: Galloway, looking pleased with himself and, for once, pleased with somebody else. As the blanketed figure of the injured customer was loaded into the first ambulance, Galloway thumped Carver's arm.

'Well done, lad. Probably saved that feller's life.'

'Thanks, sir. What about the other two, d'you reckon?'

'The Davis brothers?' Galloway allowed himself a vengeful leer. 'They'll live. Won't take the piss out of Chinamen again, though. As for you, my son, I'd say you've done enough for one day. Go on, have it away on your toes before something else happens. See you tomorrow.'

Jimmy Carver walked away with his shoulders back and his head held high, as if he were in uniform, on the beat.

He was quite looking forward to tomorrow morning.

On that Sunday morning an unwelcome face showed up once more at the station. Sergeant Cryer was about to launch into a blistering tirade when Lampton, very sober and very correct on the other side of the counter, said:

'One of your officers has stolen my wallet, sergeant. Sixty-two pounds.'

Seven

Cryer leaned impatiently over June Ackland as she tried yet again to raise PC Carver on the blower.

'Here, let me try. Carver, are you receiving me? Carver. Are you receiving me? . . . Any other unit know where Carver is?'

'What's all the noise about?' Roy Galloway strolled across the office. 'Doesn't anyone know it's Sunday morning?'

WPC Ackland made a face. 'Trouble with a capital T.'

'My little bomb hoax firm haven't died in hospital, have they?'

'Worse than that.'

'Is there anybody out there?' Cryer bellowed, as if to use his own lungs rather than the miracles of modern science. 'What's Higgins' number . . . Edwards . . . ?'

Abruptly Carver's voice came through. 'Are you receiving me, sarge?'

'No, it was the jolly green giant! Carver, get yourself in here straight away.'

Galloway looked at their faces, trying to keep it joky but probing for something else. 'That tenner you owe me isn't worrying you, is it?'

'Don't talk to me about money. That drunken bastard Lampton's been here and alleged that Carver's nicked his wallet with sixty-two quid in it.'

'Carver? Never.'

Then Cryer told him the rest of it. Stupid young woodentop, drinking with the man in a pub down the road: drinking with a man on bail. Not only that, but he had walked Lampton back home, or started out that way, anyway, just before the bomb hoax, and then left him to go to the assistance of the injured man. All that good work gone to waste! Instead of a pat on the back, there was this: a nasty taste in the mouth, and a stigma that could follow Carver for the rest of his career – if he had any career left.

'We won't know which way it's going to jump until the chief super's finished interviewing Lampton.'

'You called the chief super out?' Galloway chuckled. 'On a Sunday morning?'

Cryer could not force an answering grin. He had known Lampton too long, and knew what he was like when he was sober. There was no way he was going to have Carver suspended for something he hadn't done, so he took a chance on Chief Superintendent Brownlow being able to sort it out before it all got out of hand. Lampton had said, and was probably saying it again upstairs right now, that he had had his wallet handed back to him when released from the police station, had certainly had it in the pub, and then had been with nobody else but PC Carver. The only way he could have mislaid it, he assured Cryer savagely, was if someone had hung him upside down and shaken him, hard. Yes, he did realize it was a serious matter, accusing a police officer; but who else could it have been? Carver had walked him most of the way home, hadn't he? And what motive had he had for doing that?

All they could hope was that Brownlow was hammering home to the little soak just what damage he might do with his crazy accusations – ruining a young man's career for what was probably his own drunken lapse of memory.

The trouble was, when he was sober Lampton denied his drunkenness and denied having a soggy memory, and quenched any little fits of remorse with bad temper and vicious remarks.

They heard the door at the top of the stairs open. There was deathly silence in the office as Brownlow escorted Lampton down to the foot of the flight.

'Whitewash,' Lampton was growling. 'A cover-up.'

'I assure you there'll be no cover-up,' Brownlow said very quietly and steadily. 'But I shall see PC Carver and some of his colleagues first. Then, if I'm satisfied that a crime has been committed, I'll call in the Complaints Division of Scotland Yard.'

'Whitewash.'

The chief superintendent looked stonily at Bob Cryer. 'Can I have a car to take Mr Lampton home, please.'

They had hardly got Lampton off the premises when Jimmy Carver came in from the street, with Higgins a few paces behind him.

'What's up, sarge?'

'You come with me. Higgins, stay here in the office.'

He led the bewildered Carver away; and told him what had happened; and watched bewilderment change to horror and utter disbelief. If ever he had seen an innocent man – and he had seen plenty, as well as plenty of the other kind – this was one. But his voice hardened. He didn't want Carver to be under any misapprehensions. A rough time lay ahead in Chief Superintendent Brownlow's office, and the lad might as well be toughened up for it.

'But sarge, I never touched – '

'Just listen. The chief super's talking to Edwards, and to Higgins any minute now, and then it'll be your turn. When you get in there I don't want you being leary, right, just tell him the truth.'

'Sarge, I've never stolen anything in my life.'

'It's not what you've done,' said Cryer grimly, 'it's what they think you've done. All right, come on. Let's go up.'

For a moment Carver looked incapable of even setting foot on the stairs. Then, white-faced, he started upwards.

They stood on opposite sides of the corridor, outside the chief superintendent's office. Twice Carver attempted to say something, then licked his lips and tried again, only to shake his head despairingly.

Cryer let out a rasp of exasperation. 'I don't know what I'm going to do about you, Carver, straight I don't. I'm running out of bloody ideas.'

'Sarge, please believe me. You've got to. I've never in my life taken anything from anybody, honest.'

'If I thought for one moment you had, I wouldn't be standing here. I'll tell you one thing, though. Next time – if there *is* a next time – and you come across a drunk, you'll remember double quick that you're a policeman first and not a flaming social worker.'

'I felt sorry for him, that's all. He's got a problem.'

'No, Carver, you're the one with the bloody problem. Trouble is, you're bloody stupid enough to go and do the same thing again, aren't you?'

The office door opened. Taffy Edwards came out. He tried to give Carver a reassuring grin, and went down to relieve Higgins. When Higgins had been in to give his evidence and come out in his turn, he did not even try to smile. He looked as if someone had dirtied his hands and he wished he had never been involved in anything of this kind. It was all far too unsavoury for an ambitious young officer with a golden career ahead.

'Right, Carver,' said Cryer. 'It's all yours now. And remember what I said.'

When the door had closed again behind Carver, he could not bear the tension here any longer. They would know the outcome soon enough. He stamped downstairs.

Galloway was haranguing PC Higgins. Cryer sensed that, like himself, Galloway simply wanted to let off steam, to take it out on somebody because it was impossible simply to hang about, waiting in silence.

'Got a bit of experience under your belt now, then? Close quarters, eh?'

'Yes, thank you, sir.' Higgins was very stiff and correct. He would be.

'And when you get back to college you'll be able to write a nice little thesis on the police and relations with the public, won't you? And when it comes to malicious complaints and

63

wasting police time . . .' He swung round as Cryer came into the office. 'What's the latest, Bob?'

'Carver's in there now.'

'You ask me, I think the super would have given Lampton one hell of a roasting. In a nice sort of way, of course.'

'That won't stop him giving Carver a roasting. And not so nicely.'

Somebody rapped on the counter, and a reedy, quavering woman's voice said: 'Excuse me, officer.'

'Yeah, just a minute, miss.' Cryer slammed his fist against the partition. 'I wouldn't be surprised if that bastard Lampton's just trying to have a go. Wouldn't put it past him.'

'Hm. Don't think so. Half the time he's too woozy to think up anything like that. Too thick.'

'Just like Carver's too thick to nick a wallet.'

'Cor strewth, ain't I gonna get no service round here?'

Cryer waved abstractedly towards the counter. 'Higgins, will you see to that lady, please.'

'I only want to 'and something in.'

'We just have to pray that when he finds the allegation's unfounded, the super won't go ahead with disciplinary charges.'

'I should bloody think not.'

'Look,' said the old woman, propping herself against the counter and staring up at Higgins, several inches above her, 'I found it in the gutter . . .'

'I mean,' said Galloway, 'after saving that bloke's life in Crayford Street?'

'. . . in Crayford Street. I couldn't bring it in before, I 'ad one of me turns, didn't I?'

'It's full of money.'

'Well, of course it is. I wouldn't bleedin' well nick it, now would I? Look, what 'appened was, I was coming along from the pub after dark and I found it, see . . .'

It began to ring simultaneously in Bob Cryer's and Roy Galloway's heads. They stared at each other, and at the old woman, and at the wallet lying open on the counter.

'In Crayford Street?' Cryer breathed.

'That's what I've been saying, isn't it?'

Cryer was not a sentimental man, but he thought he had never seen a sight so beautiful as that wallet, lying there.

He also quite enjoyed the sight of Carver's face when word had been taken in to Chief Superintendent Brownlow and, after a delay during which it seemed likely that some pretty straight talking had been done, Carver was finally allowed out. He was almost as pale as when he went in, but he smiled gratefully at Cryer; and if there were tears in his eyes, it would have been downright offensive to comment on them.

Galloway said: 'You look a bit more cheerful than you did earlier, my son.'

Cryer nodded. 'Looks like someone who's lost a quid and found a fiver.'

'Hey, that reminds me!' Galloway was jubilant. 'What about that tenner you owe me? "Crack it in a fortnight", remember.'

'Trust you not to forget.'

'Come on, let's see it.'

Cryer let him see it. He put the ten-pound note down on the desk. Unexpectedly Galloway took out one of his own and set it on top.

'Right,' he said. 'Now, Carver, I want you and Higgins to go down the market. I want one of those big hampers of food – you know, full of tins of ham, corned beef, chunks of pineapple.'

Carver was beginning to look bewildered again. 'Sorry, sir, I don't get you.'

Cryer felt exactly the same.

'Your fairy godmother, Carver,' snapped Galloway. 'The old dear who saved your skin. Brought that wallet in. You don't suppose she'll get a reward out of Lampton, do you? I bet she ain't got two pennies to run together, and not a bit of grub in the house.'

'I don't believe it,' Cryer marvelled.

'What's wrong?'

'I never thought to see the day. Detective Inspector Roy Galloway, social worker!'

'Oh, piss off.'

Eight

Another week was beginning, and another mixed bag of problems could be relied on to show up. What Sun Hill station could have done without was Jimmy Draper for starters.

Quite apart from a succession of villains, there were any number of small-time regulars of one kind and another, all sent to clutter the place up: that piss-artist Lampton for one, though with a bit of luck he would keep his head down for some time to come; the old tramp who obsessively gathered up waste paper from the pavements and gutters and stank so badly that he was always being thrown off buses he had tried to board; and the old dear down Prime Street who shared her favours between the police and the fire brigade when tracking down her wandering ginger tom-cat. There was Maggie, run in by every store detective in the district after 'mistakenly' dropping two or three tins of salmon into her shopping basket, and bobbing up smiling in court to be given reprimands, conditional discharges, to be bound over to keep the peace . . . and, probably, to get away with more tins of salmon than were ever traced.

Then there were the kids. Some of the little ones managed to get lost at least twice a week, even though they lived just round the corner. They ended up in the police station while the desk phoned their parents, or the parents phoned frantically in – or failed to phone in. Sometimes Bob Cryer wondered if some folk dumped their kids near the front steps of the nick before going off to work, hoping they'd secure some free nosh and warm surroundings for the day.

This was Jimmy Draper's third visit. He was clearly enjoying it. Clearly PC Edwards was not enjoying it. Trying to get through to Jimmy's mother on the phone, he had to try at the same time to elbow the little boy away from the message pad on which he was scribbling, and to avoid droplets from the can of Coke which had been provided. Getting lost wasn't a bad idea, the six-year-old had decided.

Sergeant Cryer watched from a distance, amused by Taffy Edwards' difficulties.

At last Taffy was through. 'Mrs Draper? Good. PC Edwards, Sun Hill police station. Yes, he's been found. Pushing a trolley round the supermarket.' He smiled; then stopped smiling. 'No, I'm sorry, Mrs Draper. Much as we'd like to, we can't hold on to him any longer. We don't have the facilities.'

Cryer nodded in mocking agreement. Jimmy, with happy abandon, eyed Edwards' pen and made a grab for it. Clutching the receiver with one hand, Taffy slapped the other one down over the pen.

'Gimme,' said Jimmy.

'I'm sorry, Mrs Draper,' pleaded Taffy Edwards, 'but aren't there any neighbours who could look after your other children while you . . .' He tugged at the pen. 'Yes, Mrs Draper, we'd appreciate that.' Having retrieved the pen, he gave Cryer a thumbs-up sign. One thumb, anyway. 'Yes. Twenty minutes, then. Yes, come straight to the front desk. Thank you.'

June Ackland edged past him on her way towards Sergeant Cryer, and smiled condescendingly.

Bob Cryer wiped the condescension off her face. 'Give Taff a break from that little monster for a while. Right?'

'Right, sarge.'

She looked confident and competent. Jimmy Draper looked hopeful.

The teleprinter started rattling away to itself in the corner. Edwards thankfully moved towards it, leaving WPC Ackland to deal with sticky fingers and potential juvenile delinquents.

'Not the paternal type,' Cryer winked at June Ackland.

'You can say that again.' She watched Jimmy's hand move

suggestively towards her, not quite sure what he fancied collaring next. 'Hey, you! Sit down and behave yourself or you'll get a thick ear.'

The kid sized her up, and appeared to surrender. She sat down beside him with a shrug of accomplishment.

The teleprinter rang a summons at the end of its message. Edwards tore the sheet off and ambled towards Cryer, reading it as he came.

June Ackland winced. 'Listen, ugly – you kick me again and . . . don't say I didn't warn you.'

Jimmy grinned beatifically.

'Sarge!' Edwards flipped the teleprint in front of Cryer. 'How about this? We've got a prison escapee on the manor.' He pointed to the last cluster of lines. 'A man on the run.'

Cryer skimmed down the page, then sniffed and began to laugh. Alfie Mullins, of all people: now that was a name that never stopped haunting him. Poor, hopeless little Alfie. Just one bloody marvellous skill that had never made up for his clodhopping clumsiness in everything else. Dangerous? They must be out of their tiny minds. Poor shrivelled-up little Alfie, cracksman, peterman, call it what you liked – but a dead loss. Serving a fifteen-year stretch, and by now getting close enough to the end of it to be allowed home leave as part of the rehabilitation scheme.

But a prison escapee? Not Alfie.

'Is he *that* dangerous, sarge?' asked Edwards.

'He's not an escapee,' said Cryer irritably, 'and he's far from being dangerous. These prison staff get the shits over nothing at all. Totally misleading in Alfie's case. He's simply a "failed to return" wallah. Probably had himself a juice-up last night instead of treading the path back to his porridge. A Monday morning hangover, that's about all it is.'

Edwards looked vaguely disappointed. It sounded a lot less dramatic that way.

Cryer looked down the details of the communication again. They ought not to put crap like that on messages. Some clever-clever little fusspot thought he would get the whole

Met out on the streets to collect their poor little Alfie, wasting everybody's time while the screws took it easy and waited for the package to be returned to them.

Like hell. Cryer made a decision on the spot. He wanted no eager young copper blundering into the thing and having a punch-up just for the sake of the record. This one he would handle himself. It would be nice to get out on the old familiar patch; and he could guarantee Alfie Mullins would be back inside by tomorrow morning under his own steam.

The notion was strengthened by the arrival of Sergeant Penny. Cryer beamed. 'Just the man. Do me a favour. Relieve me for an hour?' He handed over the teleprinter message. 'I want to pop out and show young Edwards here there's more to police work than banging down doors and twisting people's arms up behind their backs.'

Penny studied the message and gave a reminiscent nod. 'Alfie, eh? We don't get that nice, shy little kind of crook any more, do we?'

'More's the pity.' Cryer jerked a thumb at PC Edwards, and they set off.

It was great outdoors. When you were pounding those perishing pavements, all you longed for was a cushy desk job: promotion, and a nice warm office and people jumping here and there when you snapped your fingers. But after long spells indoors, there was nothing like a stroll out into the sun and dust and stench of petrol, and the squad car rolling you through the streets in search of . . . well, whatever took your fancy.

They parked in a cul-de-sac on the edge of the street market. That was good, too: ambling through the market, in between fruit stalls and under the clamour of all the little shysters he knew so well – 'Look, darling, they've just fallen off the back of a lorry, and I'm not asking for a fortune . . . it's my birthday, I'm not asking one, I'm not asking two, I'm offering . . . Whoops, watch yourselves, here's the Ol' Bill.'

Stallholders waved, made a quick inspection of goods they had on display and goods they had shoved under the boxes, and yelled the usual things: 'Morning, Bob . . . how's your luck, sarge? . . . what happened to that West Ham on Saturday then, Bob? Hey?'

Cryer led the way out of the far side of the market and down a narrow lane on to a square surrounded by newish blocks of flats. They were not the depressing high-rise towers that disfigured the eastern end of the manor, but well-spaced little clusters of two- and three-storey terraces, with a few nicely angled to overlook them from six storeys up.

'This way,' said Cryer, waiting for Edwards to fall into step. 'He's expecting me.'

'Expecting you? How could he be?'

There were some things they could never be taught at Hendon. Nor would you find them in any police manual. It was something that came with experience; and experience got you angry when you read rubbish like that teleprint with its 'prison escapee' stuff and the hint that Alfie Mullins might be dangerous. Idiots like that never catered for people like Alfie. There was no in-between for them. It was either black or white; and Alfie, poor soul, was one of those grey areas. Yes, he'd be expecting Bob Cryer all right, but who else would know what they were talking about or how it came to be like that?

He remembered when he himself had first come on the manor, long before the likes of the Edwardses and Carvers and Higginses of the world came on the scene. Alfie Mullins had been a household name in those days. Brilliant: not a safe he couldn't open. Villains had queued up for his services. The only trouble was, he was tidy. His MO gave him away. He always tidied up after him: it didn't matter where he was, he always left the place as clean as a whistle. Taking a pride in his work, he got dragged into the nick every time, and usually before the shareout of the loot. The others got the money, and Alfie got nothing but the glory – and the porridge. Over and over again they tried to persuade him to shop the others, who were sitting pretty. But he never grassed and

71

always pleaded guilty. The bigger the jobs and the bigger the rake-off for his pals, the bigger the sentence for Alfie.

This last stretch had really knocked him back, though. A fifteen, and he'd never had a penny out of any of it, contrary to what other people thought – including the judge. Nor was that the saddest part, thought Cryer philosophically as he turned across the patch of battered earth which had been laid out as a lawn but had suffered from the patter of little tiny feet too regularly and for too long. A year ago Alfie had been recommended for one of the pre-release schemes: weekends at home with the family, preparation for the big wide world. His first leave had come just before Christmas. He walked out of the Scrubs that morning with his obligatory brown paper parcel tucked under his arm, and what did he find? It wasn't what it used to be. None of it. The Old Bill were no longer going about their business in long capes, riding bicycles. Villains were now well into blaggings – armed robberies. No style, no subtlety. And nobody wanted to know Alfie. The days of the cracksman were over. Sticking sawn-off shotguns under bank clerks' noses was more fashionable and a lot more effective. It was a new world to Alfie: one he couldn't adjust to. By six o'clock that evening he was knocking on the prison door, begging to be let back in.

Behind the new flats was still a colony of old, yellowing brick tenements skilfully shielded by the corner towers. As they went up a flight of steps pitted and chipped around the edges, Edwards said:

'You reckon he's still here, then? Not done a bunk for good and all?'

'Alfie only comes home because he's forced to.'

Cryer knew that, and so did the prison authorities, which was why he had to fight down this seething anger against them. Bloody liars, the whole lot of them. They knew as well as he did that Alfie had to be literally thrown out of the nick to do his rehabilitation sentence. Psychologically he feared every moment, but of course he had to go through the
72

charade of not wanting to go back, just to please his old woman.

'Sometimes,' Cryer confided, 'I'm part of a charade, just for the benefit of his missus.'

'You mean she – '

'I'm that cruel sergeant that comes banging on the door.'

'Sounds like Punch and Judy.'

Cryer smirked. 'Wait till you meet Mrs Mullins!'

They went along the landing with its rusted rail from which paint had been scaling for so long that its original colour had long been lost. The paint on the door of No. 15 wasn't so glossy, either. Bob Cryer raised his right hand, hesitated, and then banged on the door, standing back at once and waiting for the mock battle to commence. Edwards braced himself, not knowing what to expect.

Mrs Mullins was a plump woman in her late fifties who sometimes wore pink curlers, sometimes a pink silk head-scarf which might have dropped off the back of a lorry or out of a garment manufacturer's safe, and sometimes both. When she saw Cryer she showed no surprise, but gripped her flowered pinafore and stiffened as much of the flab as she was capable of stiffening. Cryer had been right: her expression confirmed that he was expected.

But the ritual had to be gone through. She said: 'All right, what do you want?'

'Morning, Eileen.' He sniffed. 'Cor! Is that eggs and bacon you've got going in there?'

'Mind your own business.'

She made a move to shut the door, but Cryer's foot was already wedged in it. 'Now, come on, Eileen. You know better than that. Don't mess me about, love.'

'Why can't you bloody leave him alone?' She made a half-hearted attempt at resistance as he shouldered his way in and past her, looking down the poky corridor. 'Cryer, you know what you are, don't you? You're nothing but a – '

'None of that. I've got a young 'un from the valleys here.

Tender ears. Not used to your kind of language. Come on now, Eileen, me old darling.'

He paced along the passageway. Mrs Mullins followed, with Taffy Edwards warily bringing up the rear. Maybe he still believed his sergeant might be misguided this time, and there might be a potential killer lurking in the broom cupboard.

Very loudly and clearly, making sure each syllable carried, Mrs Mullins said: 'You're wasting your time anyway, Cryer. He's not here. He went back to the nick this morning, like he was supposed to.'

Cryer sniffed. 'Bacon smells good. Mind if we have a look around?'

'Why bother to ask? You're going to please your bloody selves anyway.'

There was not much room for her to push past Cryer, but she managed it, storming into the kitchen and starting to clatter plates and cutlery about. Edwards, catching Cryer's eye, opened a door off the passage and peered into a tiny bedroom. There was precious little space for anyone to hide in there. He stooped to look under the bed, then came out.

On the left was the living room, with the door slightly ajar. Light flickered pallidly within, and there was the boom of television voices. Cryer pushed the door wider and went in.

It wasn't much larger than the bedroom had been, but was crowded and untidy. Dominating it was a large sewing machine, a typical rag trade piece. It was plain that Mrs Mullins was doing outside work to make ends meet. Partly finished garments swathed in polythene were draped over a shabby sofa and two chair-backs.

The television was an old model, sputtering energetically away without any visible audience. Facing it, a fireside chair was empty save for a morning paper abandoned against the cushion. A coffee table between chair and television had a knife and fork laid out on it, with a neighbouring cigarette end still smouldering.

Edwards tugged at Cryer's sleeve. Cryer feigned interest in

the screen. Edwards tugged again, mouthing silently in the direction of the long window curtains which were just not long enough to conceal the toes of a pair of carpet slippers.

Cryer raised his voice. 'Right then, Eileen. If you see him about, and I'm sure you will, mind you tell him nine o'clock tomorrow morning is the deadline. If he's not safely tucked up in the Scrubs by then, it's your door I'm going to keep knocking at. D'you hear me, Eileen?'

Mrs Mullins' head came round the door. She was wiping her hands on a teacloth, and had lit a cigarette for herself.

'Told yer, didn't I, he's back in the nick.'

'Not quite, but I'd like to think he's on his way. Don't want him losing remission, do we?'

'Come round here, threatening me . . .'

Cryer signalled to Edwards that they should leave. For a few seconds his hand rested on Mrs Mullins' shoulder. 'They're showing "The Blue Lamp" in the prison cinema again this week, Eileen.' He winked at Edwards. 'One of Alfie's favourites. Wouldn't want him to miss that, now would we?' Again he sniffed. 'D'you know, I think that's Alfie's bacon burning.'

They left under a shower of recriminations.

Back at the station, Cryer wasted no time. He put a call through to the prison, made his statement, and then listened to the sort of guff he could have predicted. He knew damn well that that oily Welsh git of a warder did not have to get the governor's permission. Yes, he knew regulations were regulations, but he knew as well that a man who had been twenty years in the prison service could organize or disorganize whatever he chose, within reason. Something could be worked out for poor old Alfie Mullins. Alfie was not a runner, and nobody thought he was.

'Yes, Mr Thomas-Llewellyn.' He played it as matey and understanding as he could bear. 'I know. It's more than my job's worth as well, but I guarantee Alfie Mullins will be back in your safekeeping by nine o'clock tomorrow morning. At the latest.' He waited, then nodded. Of course there would be a catch in it. Why did he stick his neck out on behalf of no-hopers like Alfie? It was going to cost him. 'Draw tickets?' he said resignedly. 'How many books? Blimey, you're a hard man, Thomas-Llewellyn. I hope it's a worthy cause.'

When he had put the receiver down, there was an unnatural silence. He looked around. Of course, that Draper kid had gone.

Edwards and June Ackland stared back at him.

Cryer said: 'Draw tickets! Look, how do you two fancy a weekend in Paris?'

Nine

Treffry Instruments Limited was a fair target. They had asked for it, and now they were going to get it. Colin Jackson had been nursing this notion along for some time, and tonight was the night. Redundant, they'd called him: he'd show them who was redundant. Wipe the smile off a few faces. Not a chance of getting them on the unfair dismissal line – he'd asked about that, and got nowhere – so this was the way it was going to be.

He carried three pints back from the bar and set them down on the table. Andy reached for his, and grimaced in Eddie's direction.

It was a pity about Eddie. Getting him away from that fruit machine was a big operation in itself. He went at the things with mindless determination, always managing to press the wrong 'hold', then feeding his tenpences in and getting it wrong again, until the money ran out. Whatever they got from tonight's little job, Eddie's share would be fed into this machine or one in some other pub. But he had to come along. They were mates, and it was Eddie who had put them on to that consignment of jeans in the market and tided them over for a couple of weeks. You couldn't very well leave him out.

The thumping and jangling of the one-armed bandit stopped. Eddie had run out of change. He looked hopefully back over his shoulder.

'Lend me a few ten-pees?'

'No,' said Colin. 'Come and sit down.'

Reluctantly Eddie joined them.

Andy said: 'It's on?'

'For tonight.'

'You want me to get a motor?'

'Don't need one. It's an office job – petty cash, nothing heavy. I know the place inside out.'

'Tools?' Andy was the reliable one, always able to get his hands on tools and gear of every kind.

'The way we're going in we won't need anything, but bring a jemmy anyway, just in case. There should be plenty of tools lying around inside – it's that kind of place. Oh . . . don't forget a couple of torches, though. We'd look a right load of wallies groping around with a box of Swan Vestas.'

'It's not alarmed, is it?'

'Would I take us into something that was wired up?'

Andy finished his pint and looked at the clock behind the bar. 'Half nine, then – here?'

'Couldn't we meet in the Bear and Crown?' Eddie suggested eagerly. 'They reckon there's a great new machine in the saloon there. Cops and robbers, pays out every other time.' He looked from one to the other, and his voice and grin faded. 'Oh, well. Sorry. Here, then?'

They kept it casual, leaving and coming back. Andy slouched into the bar in his usual way, looking bored out of his head, and bought a couple of packets of crisps as if to settle down for the evening. Colin noticed the bulge in the battered plastic bag he had tucked under the table, though.

Eddie, too, was his usual self. He nodded to them and went straight to the machine, taking out a fistful of coins.

They waited until he had got rid of them all. There was no way of getting him to concentrate until that was over.

Colin let half an hour go by before getting up, yawning and stretching, and saying: 'I'm off down the road. You coming, or not?'

'Might as well.'

The other two followed him indifferently to the door. Only Eddie looked back once, wistfully.

It was a walk Colin had once been used to: down towards the river, along a lane of uneven setts greasy in the dim light from a corner lamp, and then on the smarter concrete of an approach ramp. Once he had walked in through those red-painted gates every morning. Now he was redundant, and there was no way of going through the gates. He led the boys past a long wall and up a little alley which took a sharp left turn and concealed them from the road. Above were two blank walls, and one with a long window in it. Unless someone had repaired that dicey catch inside, it would be a walkover to open the upper half. He had stared at that metal frame and the bent catch God knows how many times while he stood there and peed.

'Give me a leg-up on to the sill.'

It was simple. No need for a jemmy. Nothing had been done to the fastening. One tug and he'd got it a few inches open; and then it was simple.

The three of them scrambled in and lowered themselves over the urinals to the floor. Colin moved confidently into the lead again. It was like old times, only usually there had been daylight from one end of the factory floor and strip lighting in the roof. Now only a faint hint of the sky's night glow came through the window and glass-panelled door of the office on the far side.

He moved round a silent lathe and opened the office door.

'Andy, get those curtains drawn. No cracks showing.'

He stabbed the beam of his torch towards the desk, and reached with a gloved hand for the top drawer. It was locked.

Andy muttered: 'They're not curtains, they're blinds.'

'I don't give a monkey's what they are – just get 'em over that window.'

There was the swish and rattle of the blind coming down, followed by a crash and a squeak of pain from outside the door. Colin groped for the desk lamp and switched it on, angling it towards Eddie as he limped in.

'D'you want to wake the whole bloody – '

'It's not my fault, is it? I didn't have a torch, did I?'

Colin thrust Andy's jemmy towards him. 'Here, let's see if you can do this little job without a bodge-up.' He nodded at the drawer.

It took only a few seconds. Two splintering cracks, and they tugged it open. Inside were four crumpled pound notes and a handful of change.

Andy grabbed the jemmy. 'Here, let me.' He went for the deeper bottom drawer, wrenching it out as far as it would go. It yielded up half a bottle of gin and a bottle of Scotch.

'We'd have been better off staying in the boozer till closing time,' whined Eddie.

'Why don't you stop moaning? You've been a jinx on this job right from the start.'

'Me? Now look, Mr Bleeding Big Shot – '

'You did promise, Col,' said Andy in what was meant to be a reasonable tone. 'Fifty nicker each, you said.'

'So I got it wrong. Didn't know they'd have emptied the place. Anyway, we're not finished yet.' He looked round the walls in search of inspiration.

Andy said: 'What's next door?'

Colin tried to remember. It was some kind of storeroom, he thought. Nothing big: just a small place where they kept office bills, papers and things. Or so he thought. It might have changed by now.

He flicked off the desk light and picked his way out with the torch beam raking ahead of him.

It was still a storeroom, all right; and the door was not locked. There was a smell of dust. Papers and bulging files were stacked up on metal shelving. The torchlight skimmed over them and came to rest on something square, dull and grey, but with a glint of brass here and there.

It was a sturdy old-fashioned safe.

'Cor blimey,' breathed Eddie appreciatively.

Colin checked that there were no windows, closed the door behind them, and found the light switch. They blinked against the harshness of an overhead bulb shielded only by a dusty green saucer-shaped metal shade.

'Right. Let's get that out.'

The safe was pushed well back under the lowest of a range of shelves. It was tricky to get out: Andy and Eddie had to go down on their knees at the sides, while Colin got his arms squeezed in between the shelf and the top of the safe, getting a painful grip on the back. They heaved, cursed, felt it move and heaved again. They were sweating and coughing by the time they had manhandled it out on to the floor.

Now Colin regretted not having asked Andy to bring a whole lot of tools. The jemmy was useless: it did not even scratch the paint on the old, heavyweight safe. An exploration across the main workshop produced a couple of wrenches and some screwdrivers, but nothing even as hefty as a crowbar. Heavy stuff like that wasn't much needed around Treffry Instruments.

Andy poked one of the screwdrivers despondently into the lock. Then he noticed what Eddie was up to.

'Don't you think you'd better give that stuff the elbow for a while?'

Eddie took the Scotch bottle away from his lips and wiped them. The level had gone down several inches. He looked well pleased with himself, which was more than the other two were.

'You're getting to sound like Mr Big Shot,' he sneered.

'Cut it out.' Colin sagged against the shelves. 'Start coming up with some ideas or we'll be here all night.'

'I bet there's bugger-all in there anyway.'

'Listen, you berk, there's gotta be at least – '

'Don't call me a berk.' Eddie reached up and carefully set the whisky bottle alongside the gin bottle on a shelf above his head. The gin bottle was no longer even half full. He began pacing towards Colin.

'Firms don't have safes for nothing!' Colin growled. 'Get it into your thick skull – '

'I'll do you.'

Andy moved in between them. 'Look, Col's right. We could be just that much' – he held out his finger and thumb – 'from forty grand.'

'More like eighty,' said Colin with renewed hope.

'Get that! An hour ago it was a hundred and fifty all in, if we were lucky. Now it's bleeding eighty grand. Any advance on eighty, Col?'

Colin raised his right fist, but Andy was still set squarely between him and Eddie.

'Look,' said Andy, 'there's gotta be an answer to this. So let's work it out together, right? Like a team. Let's all have a drink' – he reached past Eddie for the whisky bottle – 'and then talk some sense. No arguments.'

They all had a drink. But when it came to talking sense there was nothing doing. They squatted around the safe, examining it from every angle, and all the time it just sat there and defied them.

Andy shivered. After all the heaving and hammering a little while back, it was getting chilly in here. He said thoughtfully: 'What if we take it with us? Cart it off and work on it in our own time.'

'Where?'

'My brother's lock-up is empty at the moment. Just the place.'

'And how do we do that without wheels?'

Silence descended again. Colin put his arm across the top of the safe and leaned on it. He tried to picture them manoeuvring the safe out of that lavatory window and down the alley to a waiting van. Fat chance. It would have to go out through the goods exit into the yard. That was easy enough, but there was still the little matter of getting the gates open.

Or getting the staff door in the wall open, a few feet away. That wouldn't be so difficult from inside.

Something was nagging at the back of his mind. Never mind about a motor. There was something else. Now he'd got it in focus. On the far side of the workshop, near a flight of stairs, the torchlight had fallen briefly on a large trolley. It ought to go through that outer doorway all right. Throw a blanket or something over it, keep to the back doubles, and who would notice at this time of night?

He put the proposition to the others.

'You're bonkers,' said Eddie without hesitation.

'We'd stick out like a sore thumb,' said Andy.

'If you've got any marvellous ideas of your own – '

'Hold it,' said Andy. 'Look, if we have to do it that way, then it's got to wait until the morning. Half four, five, when it's getting light. People moving about, on their way for the early shift down the road. We wouldn't look so sussie then.'

'Not bad. Not bad at all.'

'Yeah?' Eddie looked learily at the dregs in the bottle. 'And why don't we go and break Alfie Mullins out of nick to do the job for us, eh? Bleeding bonkers, you two.'

Andy was very still. 'Alfie Mullins,' he murmured.

'Who's Alfie Mullins when he's at home?' Colin demanded.

'That's it! He *is* at home. Out on home leave.'

'I still want to know who the hell – '

'Come on, Mr Big Shot.' Eddie was enjoying himself. 'You've never even heard of the great Alfie Mullins, the great cracksman, the wonder man of all time? Not a safe he can't open. And as it happens, I know him personally.'

Colin snorted, but Andy said: 'And know where he lives?'

'He might have moved, but I could find out. Only it'll take some time. I mean, you can't go knocking people up in the middle of the night, can you?'

It began at last to fit into place. Colin and Andy would get the safe on to the trolley, and when it got light would trundle it along the way to the lock-up. That would give Eddie plenty of time to find out where Alfie was living and bring him along. Always supposing, of course, that Alfie wanted to come.

Colin said: 'Offer him a twenty-five grand cut.'

They patted Eddie on the back, and handed him the bottle for a last celebratory swig.

Dawn was making a pretty seedy job of things when Eddie drifted in through the door of the all-night café under the shadow of the old buildings. It smelt of stale smoke and stale cooking fat. Eddie was hungry, but the sight of the sandwiches in their glass cabinet did not turn him on.

83

'Just a coffee,' he mumbled.

The proprietor poured him something hot and brown. At least it washed away some of the dry, sour taste of the whisky.

Eddie leaned on the counter and said, as casually as he could manage: 'Don't know where Alfie Mullins hangs out, do you? Know it's about here somewhere.'

'Next street.' The man did not even turn round. 'Top floor of the buildings.'

'What number, mate?'

'Take yer pick from twelve.'

Eddie forced himself to drink the coffee slowly and look as if the question hadn't meant very much and might just as well not have been asked. Then he turned away. Time to get down to business.

He hadn't noticed it when he came in – there, in the corner by the door, a one-armed bandit. He rummaged in his pocket. But of course he had got rid of all the loose stuff in the pub before they set out.

The café proprietor said: 'Don't you want your change?'

There it lay on the counter: change from the quid Eddie had handed over for his coffee.

He fed a coin into the machine; then another one; and there was that lovely, bloody marvellous rattling sound, and the money was spraying into the tray.

It took him ten minutes to get back where he had started, without a tenpenny piece in his pocket. Despondently he left.

The end of the buildings was tinged by watery sunshine, but the side with balconies and front doors still lay in shadow. Somewhere a baby was squawling, and a dog began to bark. Eddie stared upwards, wondering which door he was going to select when he got up there.

A milk float clanked past him, close to the pavement. He moved hurriedly away and came to a halt on the other side of the road.

Above, a door opened.

'And don't forget to write this time. D'ya hear me, Alfie Mullins?'

A small huddled shape began to edge down the stairs. When he reached the bottom, Eddie could see that he had his raincoat collar up as if to shut out the whole world, including his wife's voice. There was a brown paper parcel under his arm, tied with coarse string.

'Good-for-nothing ponce!' It was Mrs Mullins' fond farewell as she slammed the door.

The milkman was crossing the road to another flight of stairs. Eddie waited until he was well on his way, then began to trot after Alfie Mullins.

He lost him on the next corner. Where the hell could he have got to? The road ahead was empty save for a woman swilling down a doorstep. To the left was a churchyard with its population of tilting, dead stones. But something moved between them. The path between the graves was a short cut to the nearest bus stop. Eddie broke into a run, and went in through the gate.

That hunched shape padded on ahead of him.

'Hey . . . Alfie!'

Looking neither to left nor right, Alfie Mullins wheezed his way towards the far gate. It was easy to catch him up. Years in prison had worn him down. Breath rasped in his throat with the mere effort of walking.

'Sorry to bother you, Alfie – er, Mr Mullins.' Eddie fell into step. 'You don't know me, but . . . look, you *are* Mr Mullins, aren't you?'

There was no reply. Alfie Mullins stared ahead as if needing all his concentration to get to that next gate and the steps down beside the bus stop.

'Course you are,' Eddie said breezily. 'Look, I'll come straight to the point. Me and a couple of pals, we got hold of this safe, see. Well, we can't open it. It's right up your street, Mr Mullins.' When there was still no response, he pulled the clincher. 'Thought you'd be interested for, say . . . um . . . twenty-five grand cut?'

He stopped, expecting Alfie to stop as well and face up to this terrific offer.

Alfie kept walking. Only a few yards to go now.

'What's the matter, then?' Eddie was fed up with being put down by everybody, fed up with trotting by this little zombie, fed up with every damn thing that had happened last night and this morning. 'Aren't me and my mates good enough for you, or something? Not your class, eh? Look, I'm talking to you, mister!'

He darted forward and swung to block the way. Alfie tried to nip round him to the right, but Eddie was there. Then the left, and Eddie was there again.

'Listen, Mr Has-been . . . you're coming with me whether you like it or not, see?'

Alfie Mullins did not see. He tried pushing Eddie out of the way, but there was just no way Eddie was going to stand for that. He caught the old man's sleeve, and tried to get him to shove his head up and look him straight in the eyes, just so he could see that this was business, real business.

The brown paper parcel went flying. Alfie groped vainly in mid-air for it, and slithered on the grassy verge of the path. Eddie went over with him, and jarred his arm against one of the gravestones. He heard the thud of something else – Alfie's head hitting the stone full on.

'You all right?' Eddie felt the dew seeping through the knees of his trousers. He scrambled up. 'Come on, Alfie . . . Mr Mullins . . . don't sod me about.'

Alfie Mullins was very still, with his head at an odd angle against the side of the gravestone.

Horror ran up from Eddie's damp, shaking knees to his head. It wasn't true. No way it could have happened like that. A little knock that wouldn't hurt anyone.

He stopped to touch Alfie; then straightened up again and began to run. As he clattered down the steps, an elderly man came to a halt by the pavement and began to lug his bicycle up to the short cut. He glanced idly at Eddie. Must be some night-watchman on his way home. Eddie didn't know and didn't want to know. He kept moving while the man began to wheel the bike along the churchyard path.

Ten

The probationers' classroom on the second floor had been cleared, with desks pushed to one side and two long tables laid end to end below the blackboard. Sergeant Roach dumped a card index on one of the tables and glared at two sleepy detective constables who had appeared on the scene, one still rubbing his eyes, the other hastily running a battery shaver over his chin. A telephone engineer scuttled between them, crouching as he ran a wire from a junction box towards the tables.

DC Dashwood came into the incident room with a scribbled note. 'Found him, sarge. Inspector Galloway's going straight to the scene, meeting Sergeant Cryer there.'

'Forensic?'

'They're raising a fingerprint man. Haven't been able to sort out the SOCO.'

Litten bustled in, looking hopeful and important. This was the real thing. He was prepared to add his weight to that of the CID.

'Good,' Roach welcomed him. 'Want to make yourself useful, lad?'

'Yes, sarge. But I'll have to go on patrol in about – '

'Shouldn't have poked your nose in, then. Get that blackboard cleaned, and some decent chalk at the ready. Or you'll have to stay in after school.'

The whine of a car braking heavily filtered up from the street below. Footsteps pounded up the stairs. A uniformed constable who had just plonked a pack of stationery on the nearest desk to the door was pushed aside by Roy Galloway, dressed incongruously in a hired dress suit. Roach was tempted to ask how he had enjoyed the big fight last night, and the succeeding booze-up; but then thought better of it.

Behind came Bob Cryer, in civvies, ashen-faced and with his lips clamped thinly together.

The telephone engineer was mumbling something into the handset at the far end of the table. Roach tapped him on the shoulder.

'Get lost for half an hour, pal, would you.'

When the door had closed behind the man, Galloway propped himself against a desk and said: 'First of all, unless something like your wife's having a baby or your mother's died, there'll be no time off. I want you to get that straight, right from the start. No leave until this murder's solved. Any questions?' In the face of that tense glare there were no questions whatsoever. 'Good. We understand each other. Now, what I'm going to do is tell you briefly what we've got and what line of enquiry I want you to follow. Then you'll get out there and do your house-to-house or whatever assignment Sergeant Roach allocates to you. We'll meet back here again tonight at seven and see what we've come up with. Unless there's a bloody miracle and you fall over something earlier.' His thumb jerked towards the phone. 'I want that manned non-stop. And the other one, when it's fixed. Non-stop, you hear me? If you have to go to the can, get somebody to sit here and wait. Right.' The silk scarf slipped from his neck. His black tie was crooked. His mouth was angry and even more crooked. 'I'll start by telling you a little of Alfie Mullins' antecedents.'

Dashwood handed out small notebooks, and they all groped for their pens.

Galloway summed up curtly. Alfie Mullins had left home at five o'clock this morning to catch the early bus past the prison. His route was through a short cut used by everybody in that neighbourhood, across the churchyard – a short cut for Alfie in more ways than one. One witness had already come forward from a flat in St Andrew Street, just round the corner from the churchyard, saying he had been woken by a man's voice calling after 'Alfie'. It would be too much of a coincidence to suppose that it was anybody other than the Alfie they were talking about. The time fitted Alfie leaving home and the finding of the body.

Footprints in the churchyard suggested that somebody had followed him and then walked alongside him for some yards. At some stage there had been a struggle. The body had not been moved, and all the evidence pointed to the victim being thrown sideways, banging his head on a gravestone as he fell. The assailant then ran away, out of the churchyard gate, and came close to a night-watchman on his way home from work. The night-watchman had pushed his bicycle along the churchyard path, but luckily had not obscured the footprints. He found the body, and had the sense not to tamper with it.

Unfortunately the witness claimed to be as blind as a bat. Certainly he was unable to give a description of any kind – black or white, young or old.

'What we're doing right now,' Galloway concluded, 'is searching every inch of that churchyard. Anything we find, we'll let you know. And anything *you* find . . . on the wire right away, right into this room.'

Somebody coughed. 'Could it have been an accident, sir?'

Galloway offered him a withering glance. 'This, my old son, is a murder inquiry until proved otherwise. Now, as for a motive, I want you to be thinking along these lines when you're asking your questions.' Cryer shook his head, knowing what was coming and not agreeing with a word of it. 'There may be some around here who don't see it the way I do,' said Galloway heavily, 'but I've totted up the amount of money unrecovered from Alfie's past jobs. Not to be sniffed at, I'm telling you. I know it's a long time ago, but it comes to well over eighty thousand. My intuition tells me that this is what this business is all about.'

The pattern seemed likely enough. Somebody who was no stranger to Alfie had a good idea where some of that loot had been stashed, or at any rate an idea who could lead him to it.

It was a motive far from unusual among criminals. Before Alfie went back inside, that somebody wanted a cut.

Cryer looked stony and disbelieving.

'Tonight at seven, then,' said Galloway. 'Good hunting, gents.'

He swung on his heel and went out into the corridor. Cryer was hard behind him.

'Roy, you're wrong. Completely wrong. I told you before and I'll tell you again. Alfie hasn't got a pot. Not a penny. D'you really think he'd still be living in those buildings if he had a few bob?'

'Oh, now, listen. Listen, sunshine.' Galloway's forefinger prodded Cryer in the chest. 'If you'd done your duty, Alfie would still have been around to spend those few bob, as you call them. Think about that.'

'You bastard.'

'And if I were you, *sergeant*, I'd go and get changed a bit smartish. You should have been on duty a couple of hours ago. Station officer – remember?'

He did not wait for a reply but swaggered off towards the stairs. Considering the way the poncey bastard himself was togged up, thought Bob Cryer, fuming, he was a fine one to be going on . . .

He counted up to ten and made sure Galloway was well out of sight and earshot before he clattered downstairs to pull on his uniform.

They all felt the lash of Cryer's tongue that morning. It was an unusually busy morning, which did not help. PC Carver found himself coping with two irate members of the public at one go, and had problems with the paperwork. June Ackland was handling calls at the switchboard as if caught up in some electronic game: only this was no game. A nervous PC Smith made an error in his report book, tried to alter it and made it worse, and was sent to the rest room to do it all over again, like some naughty schoolboy.

'Edwards!'

Taffy Edwards, who had hoped to slip through the office unnoticed, came to a halt.

'There's a break-in just gone in the crime book,' said Cryer. 'Round at Treffry Instruments – a factory on eight beat. The silent alarm went off last night, but there's no sign of a forcible entry. They've had a trolley nicked, of all things. I want you to deal.'

'But that's not on my beat, sarge.'

'With this murder inquiry running upstairs,' rasped Cryer, 'we've all got to be a bit flexible. Understand?'

Taffy understood. He jumped to it. The way things were today, it was no bad thing to be a good distance away from the nick anyway.

The facts at Treffry Instruments hardly seemed worth the effort. The manager, after a thorough search of the building, could report only two things missing: an old safe and a trolley. Nobody was much worried about the safe. It must have been a load of nincompoops who made off with it: there was nothing inside but a few old papers. The firm had ceased using it a good eight years ago when a new floor safe was fitted in the basement. Might just as well have thrown the old thing out while they were at it.

The trolley was a different matter. Its loss would be a nuisance to the men on the shop floor. The manager wanted the police to concentrate on getting that trolley back rather than waste time on the safe.

Edwards made polite noises and left. A load of nincompoops, the manager had said, and that seemed to figure: who else would go to the trouble of breaking into a factory just to help themselves to an empty safe and a trolley?

Colin and Andy had been hard at it for hours. But where the hell had Eddie got to?

It had proved trickier than they had expected to move that heavy trolley through the streets with its heavier load. Brute force was needed at every kerb. The wheels had a habit of slewing in awkward directions, and on one slope the whole

92

thing had threatened to run away with them. At the end of an alley a policeman had stood with his back to them for what seemed a lifetime while they did not dare to go on or squeak back the way they had come; but not once did he look round. They were exhausted by the time they reached their destination, a service road behind a parade of shops with dilapidated lock-up garages on the other side.

The one belonging to Andy's brother was a bulging mess of rusty corrugated iron, pitted with holes. There was room inside for one car, with an array of old tyres and spare parts along each wall. The edge of the door shrieked over the ground as they pulled it shut behind them. Andy groped for the light switch, and they took the blanket off the safe.

There were plenty of tools to hand, though some of them could have done with a bit of oiling. None of them proved any more useful than the ones they had used in the factory. The handle came off a chisel, Colin managed to gash the back of his left hand and dripped blood over the floor and the safe, but the safe itself resisted every attack on it.

Andy sagged down on to the trolley with his head in his hands.

Colin flung a hammer against the wall. It answered with a deafening jangle, and flakes of rust descended from the roof.

'Where the hell *is* Eddie? He should have been here hours ago.'

'It's not like him. Perhaps he can't find Alfie.'

'Or perhaps he *has* found a bloody amusement arcade.' Colin slumped over the safe. 'We can't go on like this. I've hardly made an impression on the flaming thing.'

Andy got up and began rooting about in the shadows at the back of the garage. Hope was renewed. Wrapped up in an oily rag was an electric drill. It was nowhere near being the latest model, but there was a handful of bits, and although the power point near the ground wobbled the moment you touched it, something ought to be possible.

It ought to be, but it wasn't. The twist drill made a hideous screeching as it bored into the back of the safe, and then

93

snapped. They tried again, with the same result. The place stank of hot metal, but the safe was still uncracked. They needed high-speed drills, not this grotty old stuff.

'And where the devil's Eddie?' Colin came back to the same disturbing theme.

'He should have found Alfie's drum by now.'

'I've got a funny feeling he's done a runner. You know him. Get a few ten-pees burning a hole in his pocket, and – '

'Burning!'

'Eh?'

'You said burning. That's an idea, Col.'

'What is?'

'That training scheme they put you on – that welding, right?'

'What about it?'

'You must know how to use oxy-acetylene.'

'Oh, yeah, and where are we going to get that kind of equipment this time of the morning, hey?'

Andy nodded his head wisely. 'Just so happens that there's a panel beater works two lock-ups away. Reg Atkins or something like that – got his name over the door. Fixed something for my brother once, I remember that.'

They had no trouble getting in. The hasp of the lock came away from the corrugated iron in a flurry of what looked like shreds of twisted brown paper. Andy kept a lookout, apprehensively checking upper storey windows over the backs of the shops, until Colin had lugged the equipment into the shelter of their work-place.

'Right,' said Andy. 'Now let's see what we've got.'

The torch blazed; and went out. Colin started it up again; and again it fizzled and died.

'What the hell did you do on that course?' moaned Andy.

'Well, I didn't finish it, did I? Different equipment, anyway, so don't blame me.'

'You could've told me before we nicked this gear. Somebody could have seen us. Somebody . . .'

His voice died to a whispering breath as they heard some-one hurry towards the door and then stop. Andy's fists clenched. The door grated open. Eddie was framed in the opening.

'Where've you been?' snarled Colin.

Eddie shuffled forwards. In the bleak light of the overhead bulb he looked sallow and bedraggled. 'Sorry, fellers, I . . . look, I must have drunk too much in that place, remember? Woke up on a bench down the road.'

'Bleeding charming, ain't it! And what about Alfie Mullins, our saviour? I mean, that's what you went off for, wasn't it?'

'Did you find him, Eddie?' demanded Andy. 'Alfie – did you find him?'

'Took me ages.'

'Well?'

'He's . . . got a big job on. Couldn't spare the time.'

'Did you offer him a cut, like we said?'

'Didn't want to know.' Indignation put the colour back in Eddie's cheeks. 'I had to slap him about a bit. He got a bit naughty. I might've gone a bit strong,' he added weakly.

Colin threw his hands up. 'Well, that's bleeding well it, ain't it.'

'There's only one thing left if we're gonna get this safe open,' said Andy, 'and it's gonna cost. We'll need a motor.'

They stared at him in anticipation.

Edwards was in no mad hurry to get back to Sun Hill. Coming out of the factory gates he set himself a deliberate, measured pace which would get him back in reasonable time but not expose him too soon to whatever further wrath Sergeant Cryer had in store for his men.

A middle-aged man in a dirty boiler suit slewed his bicycle in to the kerb.

'Just the thing! Guv'nor, hey – just what I need. Somebody's broken into my lock-up. Nicked my welding equipment.'

'Where's your lock-up, then?'

'Behind the shops, off the parade. Bloody sods. That's my working tools they've nicked. How can I be expected to – '

'What number?' Edwards interrupted. 'Number of your lock-up?'

'Haven't got a number. Just Reg Atkins, panel beater. You can't miss the sign.'

Edwards quickened his pace. 'I'll follow you along. See you there in five minutes, Mr Atkins. Okay?'

There was nothing to go on. The idea of fingerprints on a shambles like that was just a bad joke. Edwards prodded about inside the lock-up, and duly noted the torn-off lock, but could do little more than enter it all up in his book. Atkins had no record of any registration number on the equipment, if there had ever been any: he had picked it up second-hand or maybe third- or fourth-hand, a couple of years ago. It was hardly worth nicking, really – but for himself it was something he couldn't do without.

Edwards made his way back to the station.

Somebody upstairs was shouting along the corridor. Two lots of feet went up two flights, and one came halfway down again.

He raised his eyebrows at June Ackland. 'Still a madhouse up there?'

'Too true. I'd turn round and creep out, if I were you. Cryer's got a surprise lined up.'

'For me?'

'For you.'

Edwards carried on into the front office.

He was greeted by a wide smile – a smile from the Draper kid who had got himself lost the previous day, and looked delighted to have got lost again. Someone had tried to keep him occupied with a Mars bar, but that was not going to last more than another ten seconds.

'Come you in, Edwards,' said Sergeant Cryer with malicious pleasure. 'Just the man I want to see.'

'I'd better do my crime book entries, sarge, while – '

'A word, Bob.' Galloway leaned in through the doorway.

His gaze took in young Jimmy Draper. The kid beamed. Galloway scowled. 'Can't you get rid of that kid? We're supposed to be running a murder enquiry in this place, not a bloody day nursery.'

Cryer nodded at Edwards. 'Take the kid home. Number seven, above the shops on the parade.'

Jimmy Draper pressed a sticky, chocolatey paw into PC Edwards' hand, stuck his tongue out at Galloway, and allowed himself to be led out into the street.

'And I've just *come* from there,' Edwards addressed an unfeeling fate.

An elderly woman beamed at the pair as they went along the pavement. Probably she was filled with nostalgia for the good old days when local bobbies saw old ladies across the road and walked hand in hand with adoring little boys. Two youngsters of a much later generation whistled, and dodged away down an alley.

Edwards went up the stairwell between two sections of the shopping parade. Jimmy still clutched him tightly, as if reluctant to be delivered back to his own front door.

Mrs Draper was an unkempt woman looking some ten years older than she most likely was, but she had a ready, engaging smile and a gushing voice which was impossible to dislike.

'Oh, isn't that nice of you to bring him home, officer,'

'We were thinking of adopting him, Mrs Draper,' said Edwards wryly, 'but the sergeant reckons we couldn't afford to keep him in chocolate.'

'You see, it's not all my fault.' She caught her son's free arm and dragged him in through the door, playfully smacking his bottom and chasing him off into a room opening out of the passage. 'You encourage him down there, that's what it is. You're a load of old softies, you lot.'

Edwards thought of Sergeant Cryer's face this morning, and refrained from comment. It was safer to venture a non-committal smile.

'Don't stand there grinning like a Cheshire cat.' Mrs Draper's smile was decidedly arch. 'Come on in and have a cup of tea. I've just this minute made one.'

Sergeant Cryer's expression lingered, like the smile of the most celebrated of all Cheshire cats, on the air. Taffy Edwards told himself that he really ought to get back and really ought not to hang about here. But that face, and DI Galloway's face . . .

He tucked his helmet under his arm and walked in.

The kitchen was obviously the room where everything went on. An ironing board in one corner had not been folded up and put away, and cartons of breakfast cereal had simply been pushed to one corner of the dresser. Two toddlers were pushing each other about in a chipped play-pen. Along the window sill were some pot plants, a plastic container sprouting kitchen knives, and several matchboxes. At any rate it was a bright room, looking out over the service road and the roofs of a battered line of lock-up garages.

'Sit yourself down, young man. It's not often I get visitors now.'

Edwards took a chair to one side of the table. The sill was low enough for anyone to be able to look down on the decrepit doors across the way. Idly he watched as three youths came out of one garage. Inside was a trolley. That was all he saw before they banged the door shut.

'It's only since his father left home, you know, he's been wandering off like this,' Mrs Draper prattled on. 'We used to be a close-knit family, until *she* came along.'

There was the roar and splutter of a clapped-out car starting below the window. Still only half attentive, Edwards got up again, in time to see an old banger of a small red van drive away.

'Mrs Draper, do you know the three lads who've got the lock-up over there?'

'That one opposite?' She came to the window and stood beside him, teapot in hand. 'I don't, but I'd like to. Noisy beggars. Had me up since the early hours, they have, with their banging and drilling. Then with all those sparks flying about in there . . . Honest, what some of them get up to I just don't know.'

It dawned. Edwards said: 'You've got a phone?' Of course she had. The times they had tried to ring her and get her to come and fetch Jimmy! 'Where is it, please? Urgently!'

Detective Inspector Galloway took the call. His unwelcoming snarl turned abruptly into enthusiasm. 'A trolley? Drilling and cutting equipment? Hang on there, Edwards. Don't do anything until I get there. Five minutes. Good lad.'

In the background the familiar voice of Sergeant Cryer was saying: 'A trolley? Bet that safe'll be there too. Sounds like a job for Alfie, if he'd still been alive.'

The receiver was slammed down, and Edwards did not hear the reply, if any.

Galloway was as good as his word. A squad car was parked unobtrusively down a side street, and within another two minutes a team of them were inside Reg Atkins' lock-up. They had left the warped door slightly ajar, but even without that there would have been plenty of spy-holes in the fabric. Cryer, Jimmy Carver and Taffy Edwards were in uniform; Galloway and Dashwood in plain clothes; all of them poised, itching to go.

The three louts had to come back. The way they had left things, they had to be back here pretty soon. If not . . .

Galloway's breath hissed through his teeth like a draught under the twists of corrugated iron.

Jimmy Carver glanced at Taffy. Taffy was steamed up enough, but it was all he could do not to grin at Jimmy's expression. Oh, it was in the lad's blood all right. He just couldn't wait to race into action.

'Edwards!'

Galloway was gesturing him forward, closer to the gap in the door. That same red van was returning, bumping over the road towards the lock-up two doors away.

Edwards nodded. It was them all right.

The van pulled up. Two young men scrambled out of the

99

front seats, a third pushed the rear doors open and jumped down. Past Galloway's shoulder Edwards could see a blurred picture of some old mattresses being hauled out, then the villains moving towards the nearby lock-up. Now they were inside, out of sight.

Galloway said in an undertone: 'Right. Get ready. We'll give them a moment to settle down inside. Then box them up, nice and neat. Remember, straight in, no messing about. We can't be sure exactly what they're up to, so get 'em fast before there's any mischief. Ready? Right . . . let's go!'

They erupted out of Atkins' cramped workshop. Galloway was in the lead, wrenching open the doors of the garage. Daylight spilled in to show two of the youths packing mattresses around a safe, with the third slapping a car tyre on top to hold them down. His head came round as the officers burst in, and he tried to hurl the tyre. Jimmy Carver launched himself, cannoned off the edge of the door, and bore his quarry down in a dusty crash. The other two tried to make a dash for it, but Edwards' truncheon picked one of them off, and Cryer got the second by the arm, forcing it up behind his back until he screamed.

'One for Alfie Mullins.'

'It wasn't me.' Another howl. 'It was Eddie, not me.'

Two police cars skidded to a halt outside. Galloway slapped handcuffs on to the one called Eddie with relish, and pushed him towards PC Carver.

'Take 'em away.'

It was all over so quickly. A couple of windows high up on the other side of the road opened, and curious faces peered out, still without much idea of why three youths were being bundled into cars and why two men in plain clothes were cautiously venturing into the garage.

Galloway drew back a couple of mattresses. There was the safe; and there was a small poultice of plastic explosive tamped down over the lock, a detonator inserted and attached to a crude transistorized receiver.

'Hm,' said Galloway, pleased. Then his eyes widened and
100

he turned to DC Dashwood. 'It's remote control! Quick, get out there and tell them not to transmit on their personal radios, or they could set it off. *Quickly*, for God's sake!'

He began backing away as Dashwood raced out into the open.

'Hold it, you lot!'

One of the police car radios buzzed into life. A distant metallic voice said: 'PC Carver. Are you receiving? Carver, are you receiving? Over.'

'Don't use your radios!' Dashwood yelled. 'Don't transmit.'

He was too late. Jimmy Carver pressed his transmit button and began to answer: 'This is . . .'

He was cut short by a muffled explosion. Dashwood winced and spun round, starting to blunder back towards the lock-up.

A great cloud of dust and fragments puffed out of the open doors and wafted across the road. Scrambling through it, a begrimed shape tottered to a standstill close to Bob Cryer, who began to laugh. Then laughed some more. It could have been a tragedy, but from where he was standing it was . . . well, it was enough to make Cryer double up and hug his stomach.

There were feathers in Galloway's hair, feathers all over his shoulders and clinging to his jacket, and feathers floating skittishly all about him.

'What bloody idiot did *that*?'

Dust and feathers settled gently, soothingly over the scene.

Eleven

Everything had been pinned on the south end of the High Street three days running. Two foot patrols had been diverted so that they could cross at an angle, and a car cruised within easy reach. Unfortunately the coverage had not worked. Twice in a row the muggers had picked the north end, hammered their victims hard, and got away with it. The third day they failed to show up, but it was unlikely that they had drifted off. The tally over the past fortnight was causing Sun Hill a lot of embarrassment: sixteen cases of mugging, and twelve handbag snatches, all in broad daylight and all on the same patch.

On top of that there had been a spate of armed robberies. These looked even more dangerous, and there was a lot more money involved. After successes at two building society offices, an off-licence and two garages, the little firm involved must be getting pretty cocky.

Sergeant Cryer was not pleased. He knew he would be even less pleased when reprimands and awkward questions began raining down from above. But he refused to be panicked into changing his tactics. Lightning had to stop striking the same place. Sooner or later the muggers would surely switch their operations and see what pickings there might be at the other end of the street.

In his usual place in the parade room, in front of the usual faces, he said: 'All right, I chose the wrong end of the High Street again yesterday. But that, as they say, is how the cookie crumbles. Despite that, we'll still continue our operation from the south end for today at least.'

Jimmy Carver held up a tentative hand. 'Isn't it possible,

sarge, to get the foot patrols from beats 4 and 5 to include the north end as well? It'd take only two slight alterations to the route and then we'd get the degree of cover we need.'

'Not a point that had slipped my mind,' said Cryer hastily. 'We'll modify patrols for Bloom and Darling, Peterson and . . . let's see . . . Chilton, isn't it? And now we'll see about WPCs Ackland and Martela. Nervous, girls?'

'No, sarge,' came an indignant duet.

'Maybe our girls look a bit too hot to handle, sarge?' suggested Dave Litten. Before either of them could turn on him, he went on: 'I'm serious. Perhaps they don't look vulnerable enough, even when they're in civvies.'

It was quite a point, thought Cryer. 'Any ideas?'

'One or two.'

'And we all know what one of them might be,' said Taffy Edwards. 'Eh, Dave?'

June Ackland's lower lip grew more petulant.

'One more peep like that out of you, Edwards,' said Cryer, 'and you are in dead bother, chummy.' He nodded encouragingly at Litten. 'You come up with a good idea, and we'll see about it. Now, let's move on.'

Before he could say another word the door opened and Roy Galloway came in with a sheaf of photographs.

'Sorry to bust in, Bob, but if you're bending your mind towards those armed robberies – '

'Any minute now.'

Galloway fanned out the prints. They were black and white, in both senses of the word – blurred pictures of a tall, rangy coloured man and a stunted little white youth who seemed to like looking at the ground or away in the opposite direction.

'Dashwood managed to get these. Thought they might give us a lead.'

'Not exactly Lord Lichfields, are they?'

'The best we can get so far. You reckon they're local?'

'Have to ask the lads. Here, pin 'em up on the board. Gather round, you lot.'

Chairs were pushed back as they gathered close to the board and craned their necks to look at the fuzzy prints.

'Have a good look,' said Cryer. 'If you remember seeing either of them, I want to know. Or if you see either of them from now on, I still want to know. Only be extra careful out there. We know one of 'em is armed with a small firearm, the other with a hammer. Unless they've thought of something even nastier. So watch it. Any questions?'

They all shook their heads.

'Right, then. On your way. The great British public is out there waiting for you.'

'God help 'em,' said Roy Galloway softly.

Galloway reached the door of his office as the phone began to ring. He lifted the receiver, then edged back a pace or two to kick the door shut.

It was Tombo Robinson.

'You were right.'

'It's Decker's?'

'Sure is. And a whole lot bigger than I'd have thought.'

Roy Galloway leaned back in his chair. It was good to feel that a guess had paid off and that now there was a good chance of getting his fingers on the strings and starting to pull them.

'When can we move in?'

Tombo was wary. He had been wary all along, getting himself accepted without raising any suspicion, until folk began to talk to him freely as one of themselves. You had to listen to a bit here, a bit there. What it added up to was that there was a buzz about a really big consignment coming in early next week. No, he couldn't say which day or what time. Not yet. But it was next week all right, and once Tombo was positive he'd be in touch, they'd have to meet somewhere, and he'd sketch out the layout of the place and tell Galloway anything he needed to know.

'We could make it tomorrow?'

'We make it,' said Tombo's deep voice, 'when I'm good

and sure. I don't want no more meetings than is absolutely necessary.'

Dave Litten's face appeared at the glass partition, his fingers raised to rap on the door. Galloway waved to him to stand back and wait.

'All right,' he said into the phone. 'But tell me exactly when you'll be able to ring again. I don't want to be out.'

'Should know Friday morning. Ten o'clock?'

'I'll be here.'

Galloway put the receiver down and slapped his knee. The waiting was going to be the worst part. Now he was so close, he wanted it all over and done with.

Litten saw that he had put the phone down, and slid closer again.

'All right, Dave, come on in.'

'Hello, guv.' Litten swaggered a little, trying to be matey and respectful at the same time. 'How's it going, all right?'

'So so.' Galloway wondered what this was all about. 'How's yourself?'

'Oh, bearing up, guv. You know.'

'Well, what's on your mind?'

Litten leaned confidentially forward. 'Well, I think I may be able to help you out on this armed robbery number.'

Galloway felt a stir of distaste. He didn't like the smell of this. 'How come?'

'Well, I think I know him.'

'Which one, son?'

'Well, I'm not a hundred per cent certain, but I think I know that black bloke.'

'Have you told your skipper?' asked Galloway bluntly.

Litten retreated a pace or so, and shrugged. 'Well, no. I thought I'd come and have a word with you first, you know what I mean?'

Galloway thought sourly that he did indeed know exactly what Litten meant. But levelly he said: 'Right, hold on there a sec.' He reached for a pad and pencil. 'Okay, Dave, let's have his name.'

'Well, like I said, I ain't a hundred per cent' – Litten was getting uneasy about something in the atmosphere – 'but I think his name is Holt. Desmond Holt.'

Galloway wrote it down. Desmond Holt. 'Good,' he said. Then, ferociously: 'You didn't think you'd be scoring a few points by coming straight up here, did you?'

'No, guv, course not. I wouldn't – '

'Only it doesn't work like that.'

'I know that. I just – '

'You're out of order, son. I may not get on too well with your lot at times, but at the end of the day we're on the same side. There's a word called loyalty, and when and if you make the CID, it's a word you'll have to live with.' He looked up as another familiar shape swam across the glass, and there was a knock at the door. 'Just the man. Come in, Bob.'

Bob Cryer came in, giving Litten a sharp, puzzled look. 'What are you doing here?'

'Our friend here has something to tell you,' said Galloway smoothly. 'Now then, Dave, you tell your skipper what you just told me.'

'Well . . .'

'Hold it a second,' said Cryer. He jerked a thumb towards the door. 'I'll hear you later, lad.' When Litten had plodded sheepishly out, he said: 'Thought I'd break it to you quietly. Two gentlemen downstairs to see you. A Detective Chief Inspector Kirk, and a Detective Inspector Wheeler.'

Galloway felt winded. He had forgotten the possibility of this happening – had hoped it would go away, never come to anything.

'Thanks, Bob. Very tactful. Better get one of my lads out there to show them up.'

'Good luck.'

Roach, thought Galloway, was going to need all the luck that was going. He waited pessimistically for the two inquisitors to arrive and start the trouble rolling.

It was all so pathetic. Ted Roach's private life had often been a bit rough, especially in the months leading up to that messy divorce of his, but he had never yet let it interfere with his work. Now the wheels had started to grind just because of some stupid cow of a neighbour who didn't approve of the detective sergeant's lifestyle.

Why couldn't it just have been allowed to blow over? No one in his right mind could take that sort of thing seriously.

Galloway rose with weary politeness as the two men entered.

Detective Chief Inspector Kirk he had known and respected from way back. DI Wheeler was a different type. Where Kirk was bluff and friendly, steeped in the best old-time traditions and team spirit of the Force, Wheeler was younger and unrelaxed, showing a thin smile only when something was going wrong for some chosen victim. Together they probably made a good team for their particular job in the Complaints Division. Kirk would smooth over obvious sillinesses and put matters into sensible perspective, encouraging people to talk freely, while Wheeler waited to put the boot in the moment he saw a vulnerable spot.

'Hello, Roy,' said Kirk amiably. 'Long time no see. Sorry to be bothering you now.'

'Almost forgot you were coming. I'm up to my cobblers in it. You know how it is.'

Wheeler said coldly: 'Complaint against one of your sergeants – hardly a thing to forget. Always a serious matter, inspector.'

'There's nothing in this job that isn't serious. It's a question of priorities.'

'And you consider a complaint by a member of the public against one of your officers a low priority?'

'Not normally, but in this case it's almost laughable.'

'Laughable?'

'You know what I mean, guv'nor. The member of the public concerned has more complaints than a packet of aspirins. It's all so trivial.'

Kirk settled himself in a chair and tried to look comfortable and relaxed, though it was not really that sort of chair.

'Well, there's no doubt the neighbour is making a big thing out of this incident on the stairway.'

'She swears blind,' added Wheeler insidiously, 'that Sergeant Roach deliberately sets out to annoy her. Is there anything vindictive about him?'

'I wouldn't say so.' Galloway kept it very calm. 'He gets moody from time to time, but then who doesn't, in our line of work?'

Kirk laid some sheets of paper on the desk. 'According to this statement from this Mrs Taylor, Detective Sergeant Roach called her a nosey old cow, and told her to piss off out of it.' He allowed himself a faint, almost admiring smile. 'A very direct lad, by the sound of it.'

'He's a bloody good detective.'

'I can read. His record shows that. All we're asking is whether you have anything to add.' Kirk turned the sheets round to face Galloway. 'Read it – won't take a minute – and tell us anything we ought to take into consideration.'

Galloway had already heard the outline of the complaint when Ted Roach prepared a statement a fortnight ago. It was not going to be all that different from this bit of rubbish, no matter what'slant the woman put on it. But he made a show of skimming over the declaration.

At the end he said: 'Nothing. Just that I'll say it again: he's a first-rate detective, and this has nothing to do with his work, or with relations with the public where it *counts*. This stupid slag is turning a silly incident into a major drama.'

Kirk nodded. 'We'll drop in on her and have a chat. Often that's as far as it goes. As long as they're being listened to and they feel something's being done, they're happy. Me and my oppo here, we're dab hands at smoothing over situations like this.'

'But,' said Wheeler, 'you might just tell him to be a little more diplomatic in the future. Especially where this Mrs Taylor is concerned.'

Roy Galloway felt a tingle of relief. They were going to sort it all out. You could trust Kirk. He got up and held out his hand.

'I'll tell him that. By God, I'll tell him a thing or two.'

At the door Wheeler paused and said with apparent casualness: 'Just one small point. I was checking the duty sheets on the day in question, and Sergeant Roach didn't book off until after five p.m.'

'Legitimate overtime,' Galloway improvised. 'That would've been the week when we were up to our necks in screwings. We hadn't done all the calls. Got a couple of nickings out of it, right after this silly business.'

'Nice to see overtime showing results. Well, I think that was all.'

June Ackland and Jimmy Carver were having a quiet morning. Apart from a newsagent complaining that at least ten Yorkie bars and one copy of *Penthouse* had disappeared while his back was turned, and two women with Yorkshire accents insisting that they had got out of the Tube at Oxford Circus and why wasn't this Oxford Circus, nothing had interrupted the steady tempo of their patrol. At one end of the route laid down by Sergeant Cryer they crossed the road, turned, and kept a row of shops under surveillance as they approached the junction. There was plenty of muggers' bait on the pavement over there, from two middle-aged women with massive handbags slung from their arms as they gossiped and stared into a supermarket window, to a young mother trying to stuff change into her purse while keeping control of a child tugging impatiently at her arm. No menace was immediately obvious, though.

As they resumed their plod along the High Street, June said: 'How do you pass the time when you're off duty, Jimmy?'

He looked surprised, and went faintly pink. 'Oh . . . you know, this and that. Don't have much scope, being in digs.'

'Scope for what?'

'Well' – he carefully did not look at her – 'listening to the hi-fi, or doing a spot of D.I.Y.'

'You can always swot for something or other?'

'Like Higgins.'

They both laughed companionably. At any rate the Sun Hill team were unanimous on that, relieved to have seen the back of the ambitious, humourless Higgins.

Through a gap in the traffic June saw, way ahead, a young couple peering into the window of Barry's Antiques. The name of the shop was a lot more posh than its contents. Sid Barry had one of the finest collections of second-hand junk in the district, but he liked to keep a few nice-looking pieces in his window, occasionally attracting the attention of some wandering expert who prided himself on discovering bargains in out-of-the-way places. The couple – the girl with long straw-coloured hair, leaning against the rakishly thin boy as if oblivious to the world around them – looked more like potential buyers of a cheap second-hand double bed. A bus blanked them out for a moment. Through the rumble of its passing, June heard a thin shriek.

It was louder, more hysterical, as the bus moved past. There on the far side of the High Street the couple had abruptly come to life, turning and flinging themselves on a young woman who had just emerged from a building society office. She flailed her handbag above her head. The girl made a wild snatch for it.

'Let go, you silly cow.'

The youth brought her down. His partner kicked their prey twice in the stomach. The handbag slid a few feet away. In a second it was grabbed up, and the two were racing for the corner.

Several bystanders shouted abuse after them; but nobody made a move to intervene.

June Ackland and Jimmy Carver went skipping and dodging through the traffic. The young woman was doubled up on the pavement, clutching her stomach and moaning with a rhythmic little hiccup of breath. As June knelt beside her,
110

Jimmy Carver's radio began raising the alarm in Sun Hill station.

Too late.

Sergeant Cryer whistled up a patrol car. The hospital was alerted. In spite of the shock, the woman gallantly made a statement to WPC Ackland at her bedside. Things were not too serious: she had taken a nasty kick in the chest and another in the stomach, but there did not seem to be anything broken. She could talk, and she was willing to talk.

Not that it added up to a lot. There had already been sightings of the two muggers – young white male, young white female – but precious little in the way of positive identification. This time they had not made much of a killing. The woman had lost just over two pounds in cash and a cheque book, but she was one of the sensible ones, keeping her cheque card in her pocket, well away from the book.

'Thin pickings,' said Cryer. It was a fair bet that the animals would start again soon.

Ready to sign off, June Ackland found Jimmy Carver and Dave Litten arguing the toss over Saturday's football match. Litten was saying, 'All right, you buy me a drink on the way home, and I'll tell you just what's with the Hammers,' when Cryer's voice rang down the corridor: 'Dave – parade room, two minutes.'

The other two watched him go. He looked remarkably deflated.

'Well, now!' said June, not displeased.

'Do *you* fancy a drink?'

She studied Jimmy's earnest, apprehensive face for a few seconds, then smiled. 'Since you've been let down by your buddy – '

'Less of the buddy, if you don't mind.'

'I don't mind.'

They went out together; while Dave Litten went unhappily into the parade room and closed the door behind him.

Cryer said: 'You dropped one, didn't you?'

'Sarge?'

'Don't play the innocent with me, Dave. Look, we all know you can't wait to get out of the blue serge and start working with the superstars. But come on, why didn't you come to me about that villain?'

'I wasn't sure, sarge.'

'Cobblers. You were sure enough to go straight to Inspector Galloway.'

'I thought – '

'We know what you thought. Brownie points. Looks good on the record.'

'No, sarge.'

'Don't make it worse for yourself, son. What do you think we are, a load of old mugs or something? Loyalty, a team, all working together. That's what we're about.' As Litten wilted, Cryer let out a splutter of exasperation. 'All right, you can go. But here's something for you.' He held out an envelope which he had been holding behind his back, flicking it against his trouser-band.

'What is it?'

'Might be a cheque for your golden handshake. Or a copper handshake, more likely.'

'Sarge – '

'It's the result of your CID Board,' said Cryer, strolling off and leaving him to it.

Ten minutes later Dave Litten had tracked down the others in the pub. The two of them did not look exactly delighted to see him, but Jimmy Carver said: 'Hello, Dave, you having one?'

'I'll get them in.'

'It's my shout.'

'I said I'll get them in, all right? Bit of a celebration, you might say.'

Without asking June what she wanted, he brought her another half pint along with the pints for Jimmy and himself. When he was settled at the table he beamed at both of them, and raised his glass.

'You've had a result?' said Jimmy.

112

'That's right. Only the first stage, you know, but . . .' He shrugged. It was virtually in the bag. He knew the form. 'On secondment for a while, see how things work out. They always have to go through the motions.' He drank deeply and satisfyingly.

'Congratulations. That's great.'

Litten stared. 'You seem genuinely pleased.'

'Of course I am.'

'You baffle me, you know that? I mean, we ain't been exactly the best of pals' – he caught June Ackland's gaze and floundered – 'but . . . well, you live and learn.'

'Congratulations,' said Jimmy again, firmly.

Inspector Galloway and Ted Roach came in through the far door, looked across, and moved closer.

'All right, my son?' said Galloway. 'Happy now?'

'Yeah, well, it ain't sunk in yet.'

'Still a few hurdles to go.'

But Litten was already on his feet, trying not to make it too obvious that he was itching to desert June and Jimmy, and the whole uniform branch for that matter. As he moved away between Galloway and Roach, Roach glanced back and winked.

'He'll be unbearable now.' June Ackland's eyes looked darker and more bruised than ever.

'Give him a chance,' Jimmy protested. 'I hope he makes it. He'll make a good detective, he will.'

'Oh, yes. If being a bigot and a racist are qualifications for being a good detective, then Dave Litten's ideal.'

It rather spoilt the taste of the drink.

As she walked away alone, on her way to pick up something from the delicatessen but with her head down, brooding, June was conscious of the street noises only as a familiar, boring background. They didn't exactly hinder her thoughts, but they did nothing much to help, either. Maybe thinking was a rotten idea in the first place.

Suddenly, right ahead of her, there was a shout, the crash of a push-chair going over, and a flurry on the pavement.

'Give it up or else . . .'

Two figures had erupted from a doorway and thrown a woman to the ground. It was like a re-run – the same couple, the same pattern, tried and tested. A swift dash into action, a punch-up and a quick grab, and then away like the clappers.

Only not this time. June Ackland threw herself at the blonde and got a good lock round her neck. They crashed into the man and went down. He tried to kick June, but missed and nearly overbalanced.

The girl was cursing, spitting filth, as June wrestled her to the nearest shop frontage. The man turned on them; but then heard the shrill of a whistle and the pounding of feet. Still fighting to keep the struggling, spitting girl under control, June thankfully saw Taffy Edwards in uniform belting towards them.

The young man steadied himself, then was away.

Taffy shot past the woman.

'Police – stop!' He thrust a gaping bystander to one side. 'Out of the bloody way!'

The youth was fast. Also he knew his way around. When you planned the sort of caper he and his girlfriend carried out, you needed to be sharp on the getaway and know every gap and every side turning.

He wasn't going to make it, though. Taffy was gaining. They raced down an alley, spun round the bollard at the end, and across a street as a telecommunications van skidded to a halt. The sagging gateway of an abandoned factory yawned open before them. The man was through, racing up a creaking outer stairway, down a few steps, and across dusty, splintered floors. Taffy panted, and his shoulder bounced off a metal beam.

Somebody *had* to be there waiting on the other side. Word *had* to have gone out by now, rustling up support.

He was drawing close. Desperately the man leapt across a gap in the floor, slithered on uneven planks, and found himself at the head of a fire escape.

Taffy sprang. He came down heavily on the floor. It felt

like blotting paper. His legs were trying to run, but running on nothing. Everything came at him all at once from every angle, closing in, squeezing his ribs and lashing across his head as the floor dissolved beneath him and he went down into dust and darkness.

Twelve

Detective Sergeant Roach said: 'A sharpshooter from the Yard? What a load of old rigmarole. I'm grade A with firearms, you know.'

'Yes,' said Galloway bleakly. 'I know. But ever since that Baker Street cock-up, the people on the top floor have been playing it all very safe.'

'Baker Street was nothing to do with me.'

'No, old son. But it was very much to do with public relations. And anyway, the last thing I want is for you to have to tackle some headbanger at the wrong end of a shooter.'

'We don't even know yet if we can winkle him out.'

'No, we don't. So play it nice and cool. And while we're on the subject of public relations, it wouldn't do your career any harm to watch the way you go about your private relations. Know what I mean?'

'Yes, guv.' Roach's moustache seemed to pinch in round the ends of his lips. 'I know what you mean.'

'Right, then. And until our Wyatt Earp rolls up from the Yard, it's strictly observation as far as you're concerned. Tail this Desmond Holt character. See him sniffing around anywhere special, and I want to know. But we don't risk anything or anybody until we know what the score is, and where we can be sure of pinning him down. Him and his mate. Got it?'

'Got it,' said Roach glumly.

He was past the age when routine stuff was enough to pass the time. Sitting on street corners waiting for small-time con-men wore you down. Ted Roach was one for going in

116

with both feet. Yet here, an hour and a half after what you could only laughingly call a briefing, he and Dashwood were tucked away in a car on a grotty street waiting for someone maybe to walk past. If the villain had any sense, he'd be holding up a bank in Edinburgh by now, or drinking himself mindless in some basement club down any one of a hundred flights of steps hereabouts.

It was all Dave Litten's idea. So bloody anxious to please, that great big prawn. Feeding the boss a name, any old name, and finding what he thought might just be an address, and then letting somebody else waste an hour, two hours, God knows how many hours before they got anywhere – if they ever did get anywhere.

Dashwood turned up the volume of the car radio. A disc jockey was so busy scratching his ego that he had forgotten to put a disc on the turntable.

'Nerves,' said Dashwood.

'What?'

'My old mum reckons it's nerves when somebody can't stop rabbiting on.'

'Hm.'

It wasn't the real villains who were your enemies. The villains were your opponents, and it gave you a great lift to defeat them. It was in the station itself, among your own lot, that you found the real trouble. Being lumbered with this sort of thing, for example.

If Dave Litten thought he was going to get any help during his secondment, that help was certainly not going to come from Edward Richard Roach.

'Hey,' said Dashwood, suddenly taut.

'What?'

'Let's see if I can get a better picture.' Dashwood's camera came up slowly and unobtrusively.

'Well, well, well,' said Roach appreciatively. 'And what have we here?'

The slim, slouching yet almost elegant Desmond Holt was sauntering out of a front door on to the pavement. On the

117

scene as if popping up from one of the gutter gratings was a creepy little type who waved eagerly at Holt and then cringed, then grinned hopefully.

Dashwood said: 'Strewth. Didn't recognize him last time.' He took a picture, and another, and another. 'Known as Horse.'

'Because of his speed?' asked Roach sceptically.

'Because he's shit.'

'Don't let them see you.' Roach was growing worried about Dashwood's mounting enthusiasm for the pictures he was taking. 'Observation's no damn good if they know they're being observed.'

'Don't worry.'

'Hold it. Maybe you'd better get on the wire. Tell them we're on the move.'

The two, the short and the tall, had begun sauntering down the road. Little Horse fussed and fidgeted even when walking slowly. Desmond Holt had a lean, arrogant elegance. Following them was tricky, coasting along and hoping not to be noticed, or shooting past and maybe taking a wrong turning and losing them.

Two corners away was a little suburban grocery with a sub-post-office sign above the door and a pillar-box outside. The two men paused, stared at the sky and then at the shop, and silently consulted each other.

Dashwood muttered: 'Hey, you don't reckon they're gonna – '

'On the wire quick, like I said.'

'Uniform Oscar, this is DC Dashwood . . .'

The house in its dignified terrace had once been part of a prosperous group of middle-class merchants' homes, in those Victorian days when a five-storey building with mews for horse and carriage was both desirable and inexpensive, even allowing for the upkeep of half a dozen staff and their accommodation in basements and low-ceilinged attics. Six deep, wide steps led up to each front door between pillars
118

which had once looked classical but were now peeling like blistered flesh. Each fanlight carried a gilded number, but beside the doors themselves the numbers had been subdivided down a panel of name tags and buttons, replacing the once ornate brass bell-pull.

Before pressing the button labelled A. Taylor, Detective Chief Inspector Kirk observed that two slots above it was the name of E. R. Roach.

There was a noticeable delay before Mrs Taylor appeared at the door. One glance, and it was clear that she was the sort of woman who would keep callers waiting as a matter of pride. She must have had her clothes and makeup all fixed a good hour ago, knowing they were coming, but at the last minute there would have been the obligatory glance in the glass, the little pat to a cushion on the couch, the flick of a finger down one strand of tinted and disciplined hair, and a deliberately slow progression to the door.

'Do please come in. This door. Do go right through to the lounge.'

Her voice was high and constricted, as improbably neat as her hair. Somebody must once have told her, or she had noticed for herself, that she had what used to be called rosebud lips. She had added a touch of puce to them, and must have had one little last-minute rehearsal of that pout of mingled roguishness and disapproval.

'Please take a seat.' She waved at the chairs, each with a cushion precisely centred, and the sofa, its three cushions lined up with the same admirable precision.

'I hope this isn't putting you out too much, Mrs Taylor.'

She sighed. 'When your office rang through this morning, chief inspector, I decided to cancel my plans for the rest of the day. I thought it best. The sooner you learn the facts about that sordid fellow, the better. Now some tea, or a little glass of sherry perhaps?'

'Tea will do just fine, thank you.'

She had been prepared for this. The tray was laid, the kettle must have been brought to the boil some minutes before they arrived. As an array of biscuits was pushed towards him, Kirk said: 'Now, this statement which you made, Mrs Taylor – you haven't had any second thoughts since? Any reservations?'

'Apart from being far too lenient to the dreadful person concerned, and not caring to put every sordid thing in writing, I stand by what I said.'

Wheeler looked down his copy of the complaint. 'And you're sure of the time?'

'Oh, yes, quite sure, chief inspector.' Mrs Taylor pointedly addressed Kirk. 'I'd just rushed home from the market because I wanted to see Connors versus McEnroe on the TV. It was being televised live – the French open.'

'Three-fifty p.m.?' said Wheeler knowledgeably.

'Give or take a minute, yes. Yes, it would be. I just arrived at my front door, when that man and his trollop were coming down the stairs. She, I might add, was nearly naked.' Mrs Taylor's nose wrinkled. 'Just a tiny little bikini bottom and a very thin see-through top. Quite disgraceful.'

Kirk and Wheeler exchanged covert glances over the rims of their cups. Kirk said: 'Can you tell us precisely what led to the argument?'

Mrs Taylor waved towards the window. The two men got up and looked out. Below, within a sheltering quadrangle of terraced houses, was a communal garden. A number of individual gates led in from individual blocks, and there was a larger gate opening on to a lane at the end. Flower beds and clusters of shrubs marked the perimeter, and a number of trees had been set with careful irregularity over the grass and near the central junction of two diagonal paths. It looked very tranquil, a pleasant oasis in the heart of busy streets, shops and run-down hotels.

'I have lived here a great number of years.' It had all the makings of a speech which Mrs Taylor had rehearsed any number of times. 'Fifteen years, in fact. All the tenants know me, and they all know how I am if I sit in the sun too long. It
120

brings me out in a hideous rash. So I always have to sit in the one spot. It's the only shady spot in the whole garden.'

'Prickly heat,' commented Wheeler.

'I beg your pardon?'

'The rash, madam. It's called prickly heat.'

Mrs Taylor's nose wrinkled again, with growing distaste. 'Oh, no. No, indeed. This is something quite different.' She moved back, agitated, to the tea tray.

Kirk prompted: 'And Sergeant Roach made the mistake of occupying your chair one day?'

'Oh, no, chief inspector. Not your rude young sergeant, though I wouldn't have put it past him. It was his trollop. Lounging in my chair, flaunting herself. You do realize, of course, that they're not married?'

'Yes, madam, we are aware of the fact. What happened then?'

'Well, I went across and asked quite politely to have my chair back. You should have seen the look on that girl's face! She let me have my chair back, but I could tell she resented it. You only had to see the look in her eyes to know.'

'But nothing was said?' Wheeler interposed. 'No argument or anything?'.

'No, there was not. But from that moment on your sergeant has done nothing but be rude to me. He takes every opportunity of deliberately upsetting me.' She leaned forward to command Kirk's attention. 'You realize he comes home all hours of the day and night?'

'Being a detective sergeant in the Met police, Mrs Taylor, he would. He has to work all sorts of strange hours.'

'But when he comes home at three o'clock in the morning and *deliberately* uses the toilet in the noisiest way possible . . . ! I know it sounds silly, but he does, and he does it on purpose.'

Wheeler was intrigued. 'How do you mean, madam?'

'He lives directly above me.' She stopped, making a little *moue* and looking away at one of the plaster ducks on the

121

wall, apparently preparing itself for a nose-dive into the illuminated fish tank.

'Please, Mrs Taylor,' said Kirk gently, 'you can tell us. No need to feel embarrassed.'

'Very well, if I must. When he . . . when he . . . pees, he does it right down the middle, right into the water. You can hear everything down here. Everything.'

Kirk preserved a suitably grave countenance. 'Most annoying, I'm sure. But now, getting back to the row on the staircase – what exactly happened?'

'Well, as I've explained, I'd just arrived home when they were coming down the stairs. And I might add that he was nearly as naked as she was. Just a tiny little pair of shorts. I merely asked him not to sit on my seat in the garden, that's all. Well, he got angry and started calling me names. He called me a . . . a silly cow, and when I said I'd complain he told me to . . . well, he swore at me.'

'Tell us what he said, please, madam,' said Wheeler.

'He told me to piss off,' said Mrs Taylor with sudden force. 'The man has a foul mouth.'

She looked triumphantly from one to the other. This, so far as she was concerned, was the clinching proof of the whole deplorable affair.

Kirk put his cup and saucer down on the lace runner lying across the tiny table beside him. 'Could you tell us why you asked him not to sit in your seat in the garden, Mrs Taylor?'

'I was thinking of sitting there myself, chief inspector. As I said, it's the only spot I can sit in with any comfort on a sunny day.'

'Do you have a portable television set?'

She blinked. 'Portable television? No. Why do you ask?'

Wheeler, who had seized the point, edged forward in his chair attentively.

'I thought you mentioned earlier that you'd rushed home from the shops in order to watch tennis,' said Kirk. 'Having a portable television set would have enabled you to do both. Sit in the garden *and* watch the tennis.'

Mrs Taylor wriggled uncomfortably. 'I see. Well, I intended going down after the tennis, straight after the match in fact.'

'I see.' Kirk began to get up. 'Thank you very much, Mrs Taylor.'

'That's all you want to ask?' She glanced round at all her tidy preparations, regretting that they had been on display for such a short time.

'I think that's all, thank you.'

'And something will be done?'

'I can assure you that we'll do all that is best in these distressing circumstances.'

Mrs Taylor's lips compressed into a satisfied blob.

Walking back down the steps to the street, Wheeler said with a certain dour satisfaction of his own: 'She's not going to let it drop, sir.'

'No, I can see that. And I can see why Roach doesn't get along with her. Don't see why we should feed her with her whole pound of flesh, though.'

'The trouble is, it's no longer just a matter of what *she* wants.' Wheeler glanced sideways at his colleague. 'There was something she said – '

'The time of day?' said Kirk sadly.

'That's right. Lined up against Roach's time sheets, I can't say I like the look of it.'

'Shame. Good man, good record.'

All the signs were that Holt and Horse meant business. A cheeky pair, you had to give them that, operating this close to their own doorstep. Now they sauntered into the post office, a few yards apart, not swapping another glance.

'Stay with the car.' Roach eased himself out.

'But look, sarge, if the two of them – '

'I'll send a recorded delivery postcard if I need you.'

Ted Roach crossed the road as casually as the two men had done. Desmond Holt, picking out a birthday card from the rack and putting it down again, looked warily at him as he entered the shop but made no other move.

An elderly man was shuffling away from the postal counter grille. Roach took his place. 'Er, could I have some . . . er . . . postal rates leaflets, please.' He waited, tense with the strain of not looking round, as the leaflets were handed over. 'Thanks. Oh, and while I'm at it, could I have . . . um . . . twenty-four first-class stamps as well, please.'

Holt's patience snapped. Suddenly he had crowded Roach out of the way, throwing him back towards Horse; and there was a gun in his hand, jabbed across the counter at the cowering man on the other side.

'Right.' The gun flicked towards Roach and flicked back again. 'You, keep quiet. *You* . . . pass the money over. All of it. And move it.'

'Do as he says' – Roach had his eye on the gun and Holt's panicky trigger-finger – 'for God's sake.'

'Shut up or you're dead,' snarled Holt. 'Just shut up.' With his left hand he hammered on the counter. 'You an' all, if you don't get a move on.'

Faintly, in the distance, Roach heard the mellow music of a police car siren. Was it coming this way, or heading for some other incident, somewhere else?

'The Bill!' squealed Horse.

Holt swung round to glare at the door. The man bending down, shaking, towards the safe made a suddenly wild, courageous gesture. His foot kicked out, and an alarm bell began jangling outside the building.

Holt cursed and raised his gun.

'Hold it,' said Roach. He fended Horse off with one elbow. 'Police officer.'

'That so? Then out of my way, man, or I'll top yer. I mean it.' Torn between the man now cowering on his knees behind the counter and Roach's burly shape, Holt advanced on Roach. 'You move, and you're dead.'

Horse made a run for it. He had reached the doorway when Dashwood came in fast. All at once there was a hammer in Horse's hand, lashing out and taking Dashwood on the shoulder. Roach went in low, catching Holt around the waist

124

and flinging the two of them against a narrow display cabinet which rattled and tinkled like a job lot of door chimes. Holt began beating him about the head with the gun butt, and brought his knee up. A sharp corner of something solid and unyielding caught Roach across the corner of the mouth, but he made one last mighty heave and sent Holt sliding in one direction while the gun rattled away in the other.

Then the shop was full of uniformed officers. Two of them hauled Holt to his feet. Another looked down at Roach and Dashwood, slumped against the display rack, getting their breath back.

'You all right, guv?'

'We'll live.' Roach dabbed at something sticky and smeary on his chin, and found that blood was oozing from the side of his mouth. He edged himself a few inches to the left and groped for Holt's gun. Then he began to laugh helplessly. 'Bloody hell, would you believe it?'

'No need for that sharpshooter now,' said Dashwood admiringly.

'Never was.' Roach dangled the gun in front of him. 'Look at that. It's only a toy!'

Thirteen

First they laid two long metal ladders side by side across the surviving joists of the shattered floor, then began hauling lengths of rope along them, together with what looked to Bob Cryer like a bosun's chair. The fire officer in charge stooped over the hole with its pile of rubble and clicked his teeth ominously.

'There could be a ton of the stuff on top of him.' Straightening up, he glanced past the sergeant. 'That one of your lads back there?'

Jimmy Carver was standing well out of the way of the firemen as they cautiously tested the fringes of the floor and eased tackle into position.

'One of his mates,' said Cryer.

'He's looking pretty pale. May not be a pretty sight, when we scrape it out.'

Cryer stepped over a coil of rope and made his way to Carver's side. They watched as two firemen lowered themselves with infinite care over the jagged rim of the hole, testing beams that had sagged sideways, and guiding a grapple to the centre of the mess. Cryer longed to get in there with his bare hands, manhandling the muck out of the way while there was still a chance that Taffy Edwards might be breathing. It didn't seem likely, but those boys knew what they were doing and they were taking no chances.

Cryer said hoarsely: 'PC Carver, you can get back to the station and relieve Litten. Or the other way round. He can come and spell you.'

'I'd rather stay, sarge.'

'Look, lad, this may take hours, and it could be a bit nasty.

For your own sake, I'm ordering you . . .' But he looked at Carver's face and let the order fade out.

'I'd rather stay, sarge.'

'Yes, I thought you would.'

Some splintered planking and a baulk of timber were heaved out and swung to one side. A hastily mounted light was dragged to a perilous angle above the hole, and a fireman with a heat-seeker probed through the rubble below for the evidence of Taffy's body.

'About there . . .'

Another man lowered himself over the edge, bracing himself against two splayed beams, and lifted, backbreakingly, a plank and then another one.

The brigade officer, as eager as Cryer to get his hands on something, to *do* something, grabbed one of the torches and shone it down past the gingerly working fireman.

Something sharply rectangular, dully gleaming, rested in an angle of grimy woodwork.

Cryer, venturing towards the edge, said: 'Oh, Christ.'

It was Edwards' radio.

'Hang on!'

The fireman shoved aside a thin but solid segment of boarding. It had been resting on two beams which had collided into a crosspiece, sheltering a small, unharmed space below. In the space, smaller than that of the smallest tent, lay Taffy Edwards. A few inches away, the crushed edge of what had once been his helmet protruded from a lethal tangle of bits and pieces. But Taffy was clear of any weight. As the light sought him out, the mask of filth on his face cracked and began to dissolve. He raised one arm, showering dust, and moaned.

'I'll be buggered!' said the brigade officer joyfully. 'Just look at that!'

Taffy opened one bleary eye, and began to cough.

'Anybody got a plaster?' he wheezed.

The return to Sun Hill was jubilant, and the reception there swelled into a double celebration. Roach and Dashwood,

127

looking decidedly battered round the edges but strong enough to stand up to the fusillade of jokes, were knocking back tea in vast quantities and ready to cheer anybody and anything.

'Nice work . . .'

'What a day!'

'Hero of the hour!' Bob Cryer seized Roach's hand, and two of the WPCs began to cheer.

'Come on, come on,' groaned Roach. 'Shut up, you wallies. Routine stuff, and you know it.'

'Oh, hark at Mr Modest, eh?'

'Anyway, it wasn't a real shooter.'

Jimmy Carver, unable to stop smiling and tugging at his ear, and then laughing and fiddling with a button, bubbling over with joy, said: 'But you weren't to know that, were you, guv?'

'Of course I knew it. What do you think I am – silly?'

Roy Galloway came down from Chief Superintendent Brownlow's office to join in the general hubbub of mutual congratulation.

'The super wants a word with you in five minutes, Bob.'

'Probably about our friendly neighbourhood mugger.'

'You got him as well? In spite of Taffy – '

'We got him,' said Cryer. 'One minute later, to be precise. Found himself up against a nice big gate with a lot of wire mesh in his face.'

'Oho. Like that? Short riot?'

'Let's say he just got a slap.' Cryer decided it was time to restore order to the place. 'Right, what about showing some faces on the street? And Litten, don't you go scarpering off with your new chums until you've filled in those sheets in there – every last one of them.'

It took just twenty-four hours for the cloud to drift over that sunny sky. Reporting in next day with a sore mouth and a slightly sore head from an evening's celebration, Ted Roach was otherwise in a good mood. It was still good when Galloway said: 'Super wants to see us, Ted. At the double.'

'I was going to get my hair cut.'

'And say thank you nicely,' Bob Cryer suggested, 'when he pins the medal on.'

'I can hang it up with the other two, and my divorce papers. Oh, and the red letter from the mortgage company.'

He noticed that Roy Galloway was silent as they went upstairs, but for himself he had no forebodings. And it did start out pretty well. The moment they were in Brownlow's office, the chief superintendent said briskly: 'Sergeant Roach, I have just been reading the arrest report on Desmond Holt. Inspector Galloway has recommended you for a bravery commendation.'

It was no good joking about it. It did mean something. It meant a hell of a lot. 'Thank you very much, sir.'

'In the circumstances I can only say that I am going to endorse his recommendation. However, that is not the only reason for your presence in my office this morning.'

'Sir?'

Brownlow could not sit still. He got up and paced round his desk like an animal seething with a rage to spring. 'Sergeant Roach, are you aware that as a result of a complaint by one of your neighbours you've laid yourself open to a charge that's tantamount to stealing?'

Roach's stomach turned over. It was impossible. But from the corner of his eye he was aware of Galloway standing stiffly beside him; and Galloway's face was grimly set.

'Sir, I don't understand.'

'Don't you? Look, this complaint by that Mrs Taylor of yours – '

'She's certainly not mine, sir.'

'Shut up, sergeant,' growled Roy Galloway.

'In normal circumstances,' said Brownlow, 'this might be simply a case of smacking your wrists and telling you to watch your conduct in future. That's the way we'd like to handle it. But since Chief Inspector Kirk's enquiry it's no longer that simple.'

Roach wanted to speak, but decided not to.

'Since that enquiry,' Brownlow went on, 'there's every possibility that you could be suspended from duty and charged forthwith. As a result of your bloody stupidity you could have washed all the good work of twenty years down the drain – twenty years of loyal, dedicated service.'

'But what's this got to do with stealing, sir?' The room seemed to be spinning round. It couldn't be real. 'I haven't stolen anything.'

'You stole *time*, sergeant. Time is money. The taxpayer's and ratepayer's money. You still don't get what I'm talking about?'

'No, sir.'

'On the 31st of May you had a ruckus with your neighbour, Mrs Taylor, right?'

'Yes, sir, but I don't see – '

'We have Mrs Taylor's statement, and confirmation from two other neighbours who heard the altercation, that it took place on the staircase between three-fifty and four o'clock that afternoon. Also you were dressed in a manner which suggested that you were about to do a spot of sunbathing. So, too, was your young lady.'

The cloud darkened, but now Ted Roach began to see its outlines. Now he knew what the chief superintendent was talking about. It was worse than anything he could ever have expected.

'At the time of that argument, sergeant, the British ratepayer was paying you overtime. You were logged as being on the other side of the bloody district. You should not have been anywhere near home at the time in question. Do you understand *now*, Sergeant Roach?'

Roach hardly recognized his own voice. It scraped and rustled in his head. 'Yes, sir. I get it. I can only say, sir, that at the time I was under a great deal of stress.'

Galloway said: 'I'd like to confirm that, sir. We were at it every hour of the day and night, straight up. And we did get a result on all those break-and-enters.'

'I've made every allowance for that. It doesn't alter the fact

130

that you cheated by making an entry for that afternoon which showed you booking off at five-thirteen.'

It was more than Roach could take. 'Look, sir, what about all the hours I did do overtime and I never booked for them? God knows how many hours. What about *them*?'

'I am not interested in what has not been logged,' said Brownlow, 'only what has.' He spared one furious glance for Galloway. 'You've been a DI long enough, Roy – how the hell did this get past you?'

Familiar sounds welled up from the rooms and corridors below. Slamming of doors, a burst of laughter, a bell ringing somewhere. There was the reassuring swish of traffic outside, and a rumble in the wall which had something to do with the plumbing, and had been like that for at least five years now. Yet the room was suffocated by silence.

Roach stood quite still, waiting for the worst.

Brownlow leaned back against the edge of his desk. 'This is what saved you, Roach. The Complaints Division, having taken your full record into consideration, have decided to give you the benefit of the doubt. The matter of disciplinary proceedings has been left entirely in my hands. Consider yourself very lucky this is going to go no further.'

'Thank you, sir.' Roach just managed the words.

'You'll be informed in due course what disciplinary measures I do intend to take.'

'Sir. Thank you, sir,' said Roach again.

He and Galloway went down the stairs in bleak silence, almost as bad as the one that had clouded the office for an endless minute.

'Now that's over,' said Galloway in his most clipped tone, 'we'd better call in on your pop-gun pal.' In the office he stopped, half crouching in that predatory way he had. The mateyness, camaraderie, call it what the hell you liked, of the day before seemed to have been sucked up into that dark cloud hanging over Sun Hill. 'Sergeant Cryer!'

'Anything I can do to oblige?'

131

They were like two cats trying out their voices before they unsheathed their claws.

'Our friend from yesterday. Properly charged?'

'You know damn well he was.'

'Proper warnings?'

'We don't do it any other way.'

'And we can see him? Have a little encouraging word with him?'

'Wouldn't mind being there, just to check on it.'

Galloway thawed. 'Oh, come on, Bob. Let's go see, before he goes up. See if we can make the stupid sod see some sense.'

The three of them went into the interview room, and were waiting when Desmond Holt sidled in. A night in the cells had made little difference to his loping gait, and the constable who shepherded him along might just as well not have been there. Holt had his own image of himself, and it had not yet been shattered.

'Sit,' said Galloway.

Holt sat in the straight-backed chair as if it had belonged to him all his life. His dark eyes and dark lips were beautifully shaped – and contemptuous.

'Your so-called mate seems to have legged it,' Galloway proceeded. 'He's left you right in it.'

'Dumped you,' Roach contributed. He was in a right good mood to contribute anything, to work a lot of things out of his system.

'He's a shitbag.'

Holt favoured them with a drowsy, faraway smile. 'That's the way it goes, isn't it?'

'You're at a disadvantage.' Galloway hitched himself across a chair and leaned on its back, peering up at Holt in commiseration. 'Good-looking boy like you, I mean, really! Coloured, too.' He allowed himself a glance at Bob Cryer. 'He's on a loser or what?'

'Just a bit.'

132

'They don't have a special place to protect boys like him inside, do they?'

'Not that I've heard of.'

'All slim and lovely, eh? He won't come out the way he goes in, that's for sure.' Galloway scraped the chair round some forty-five degrees, and hit out: 'Now, I'm going to put something to you, and I'm only going to say it once, so you listen. And you listen good. You tell me where your mate's likely to have legged it to' – he tried a confidential wink and bob of the head – 'and maybe I'll have a little word with the beak for you tomorrow.'

'Yeah. Yeah, 'course you will.'

'Oh, come on,' Roach crashed in. 'You owe him nothing. He dumped you, left you to carry the can all on your own.'

They waited. Holt kept them waiting. When he raised his head, his liquid brown eyes were swimming with something that blended poison and defiance.

'I got nothing to say. I don't know where he'd be.'

'All right, my black friend, you want to play it that way, that's up to you.'

There was a tap at the door. Sergeant Penny came through with a message slip. Roy Galloway took it in at one glance, and then raised his head complacently.

Holt said: 'Don't try it on. I've seen cons before.'

'You have, son? Okay. Take him down, sergeant. You blew it, son. Blew a chance of having a friend in court tomorrow. Only now it's too late. Your pal Horse got picked up by the Essex police half an hour ago.'

'Like I said' – Holt's stubborn gaze did not waver – 'it's the way it goes, isn't it?'

Galloway nodded at Cryer. The sergeant and the officer propping up the door jamb moved in and stood on either side of Desmond Holt, whose limp indifference was an insolent challenge in itself.

He looked gloatingly at Ted Roach. 'The way it goes, eh?' Abruptly he brought his right hand up, two fingers projecting like a kid's fingers, playing cops and robbers. 'Bang, bang!'

133

Roach was halfway across the room before Galloway caught him. Bob Cryer raised an eyebrow, and shifted Holt out of the place at a rate of knots.

'Bastard!'

Galloway said: 'Temper, Ted! I'm beginning to feel a whole lot of sympathy for that poor Mrs . . . what was her name?'

'Mrs Bloody Taylor.'

'I wonder who christened her that?' As they left the room into the clean, dank, featureless corridor, Galloway added: 'Ted, what *were* you doing in that garden that day?'

A reminiscent gleam came into Ted Roach's eyes. 'It was a very warm day, guv'nor. Very warm indeed.'

Fourteen

Maggie was back. Murder and mayhem might come and go. Grotty little villains with lengths of lead piping and bits of bent wire to open car doors might put in an appearance and then disappear on to fresh patches. Maggie Drew came; and kept coming. The officers of Sun Hill police station felt that Maggie was likely to go on for ever.

This time it was WPC June Ackland who had made the arrest. Maggie had come bumbling out on to the pavement outside the supermarket, blinking in the sunlight and looking just like any of the rather vague, doddery old women who did their shopping along the street and tottered back to their cramped little rooms to sit in front of the telly or babble incessantly to the budgerigar. But she was not like all the others. Fate – and the store detective – had singled her out. Maggie had taken only a few steps away from the glass doors when a hard-jawed middle-aged woman caught up with her and brought her to a halt. As they argued, the store detective held up a peremptory arm, and June Ackland crossed the street to join them.

Maggie blinked owlishly from one to the other, shaking her head in pitiful disbelief.

Ackland said: 'Salmon?'

'Salmon,' said the store detective. She held out a cold, bony hand. 'Newnham, officer.'

'Miss Newnham – '

'Mrs.'

'Mrs Newnham, you're proposing to make a charge?'

'Not for the first time. For all the good it's done, the last few times,' added Mrs Newnham frostily.

135

'Come on, Maggie. You'd better come along to the station and tell us the tale. And you, Mrs Newnham, will you come and make a statement, please?'

'I'll be glad to.'

Maggie stood where she was, sucking her lips in and digging her right thumb into the handle of her shopping bag. Then she seemed to wake from her trance, and opened the bag to peer in.

'Well, I never!'

'But you did,' said Mrs Newnham. 'Over and over again.'

'Salmon!' marvelled Maggie. 'A tin of salmon! What must have happened, now I come to think about it . . . yes, that's it . . . I put the tin in my bag by mistake. My bag was in the trolley, see, and I wasn't looking where I put the tin. Now, that's a mistake anybody could have made. Couldn't they?' she appealed to them, with a sweetly reasonable smile.

'Anybody,' Ackland agreed. 'But not eight times in the last twelve months.'

Looking pathetically downtrodden under the harsh weight of the injustice which was being visited on her, Maggie was led away in the direction of Sun Hill. When the contents of her tatty shopping bag were tipped out on the desk, Sergeant Cryer looked almost as disbelieving as she was trying to do.

'Not salmon again?'

'Sergeant, I been trying to explain what an innocent mistake – '

'I bet you've got more tins of salmon at home than John West,' Cryer marvelled.

June Ackland tucked herself into a tiny cubicle with Mrs Newnham and began laboriously to write out the store detective's statement. There ought to be a duplicated version of it, she thought, with a few gaps for the necessary names, for in every other detail it was wearisomely the same as so many other shoplifting incidents. Store detective observes suspicious movement behind row of shelves; notices bulge in shopping bag before contents of trolley have been paid for and stowed in the bag; suspect leaves checkout point and
136

proceeds to exit doors; is on her way out and along the street when challenged . . .

Cryer put his head round the door.

'Sarge, Mrs Newnham, store detective, Hartfield supermarket.'

'We do know each other.' Cryer was unusually curt. 'Your company prosecuting, are they?'

'Company policy. The way things are nowadays, we have no choice. No matter how little the value, or the circumstances of the offender.'

Cryer nodded at WPC Ackland. 'Add that to the end of the statement. All right?'

Mrs Newnham's austere features stiffened into those of a hanging judge. 'I can see you're not very happy about that.'

'I'm always happy, Mrs Newnham. Just that I want the magistrate, the public in the gallery, and the press . . . I want them all to know your company's policy.' June Ackland knew, if the other woman did not, that Cryer's tongue was firmly lodged in his cheek. 'A deterrent, you see.' As he began to close the door, he added: 'When you're ready come right out and I'll charge her.'

It presented quite a cosy scene when Ackland and Mrs Newnham did emerge. Cryer had a charge sheet and a cup of tea on the desk before him, while Maggie sat on the bench wrapping her fingers round a plastic cup and whimpering spasmodically at the heat.

'Why don't I get a cup and saucer no more? I remember the time when you could get a decent cup of tea in this nick.'

'Safety regulations, Maggie.'

'Safety? You don't think I'd try and do meself an injury, do you?'

'Not your safety, Maggie. Ours. Can't afford to have our cups and saucers disappearing into that bag of yours.'

As Mrs Newnham prepared to sign the charge sheet, June Ackland put the groceries one by one back into the bag. Maggie watched her tin of salmon with distant yearning.

Roy Galloway came clattering down the stairs. Maggie's face brightened immediately. 'It's Mr Galloway!'

Halted on his way to the outer door, Galloway looked at the desk. 'You again, Maggie? Not tins of salmon?'

'What else?' said Cryer.

'Cor, you must have more tins of salmon at home than – '

'She's already heard that one, Roy. Where are you off to in such a rush?'

Galloway imperceptibly shook his head, a warning not to push the conversation too far. 'Just a contact. I might have a job on tomorrow. Tell you what it's all about later.' He nodded at Ackland. 'Get the girls to bring in some civvies. Stuff they don't mind getting dirty. And Dave Litten as well.' As June Ackland raised her head over the shopping bag and lifted it from the desk, he added: 'A rehearsal for the station pantomime.'

'Shouldn't think your department would want any practice,' said Bob Cryer.

Galloway's lip curled, but he did not hang about to think up a retort.

Tombo Robinson had once done some training on his own account down on the running track of this local stadium and had made quite a reputation, even if it lasted for only a little while, in the 800 metres. Now younger and fitter lads were training down there. Tombo and a couple of friends from the Clayview estate still devoted some hours each week helping and encouraging the youngsters, and arranging a number of regular functions for them. He was a familiar figure on the ground and the stands, coming and going as he pleased, adding a darkly benevolent presence to the scene. Sometimes friends would be with him, sometimes he sauntered in alone to enjoy the spectacle. Today he was alone; but not for long.

Roy Galloway ambled down the aisle and worked his way along the row. When he sat down, Tombo kept him waiting while he rolled a cigarette. Then Tombo said:

'You didn't really know for sure, did you? About Decker's?'

138

'Not right at the start, no. Not one hundred per cent.'

'Oh, it's a hundred-per-cent set-up all right.' Tombo stared gloomily out over the stadium. 'They've got some real professionals backing them. People way up the line. Big time, big business, big money. Not your ordinary man on the street, Roy, pushing bits here, bits there. I'm telling you, man, this is the real McCoy.'

Galloway whistled faintly and thoughtfully between his teeth. 'If it's that big, d'you think I should hold off for a few days, keep it under surveillance, wait till we can be dead sure of making a killing?'

'Might suss you out. And me.' Tombo inhaled and stared unhappily ahead still, as if one glance at the detective inspector might let him in for more trouble. 'The sooner I'm out of that place, the better for my health. It hasn't been easy.'

He had made no great show of trying to get himself into the old, boarded-up cinema. It took an apparently chance meeting with one of his old cronies who had found himself a job as one of Decker's minders. Still not pushing it, Tombo had talked idly about the old days, and waited to be invited to try the new premises inside. He acted dumb, but let himself be coaxed – watched all the time by a white heavy, Pat Corcoran, who he could tell didn't trust him. But then, it took only a little time to discover that Corcoran trusted nobody. It wasn't his job or his nature to trust folk.

Inside, Tombo explained to Galloway, the auditorium was pretty much the way it had always been, but rooms and offices opening off the circle had been tarted up as plushy little hideaways where you could take a fix, smoke grass, or try anything else that took your fancy. Once you were there, Decker's boys could provide you with many a thing to take your fancy. The upstairs foyer had been converted into a bar, with reggae music part of the time and drowsy, insinuating stuff when the mood was right. And there was a corner bar where you bought not just what you wanted but what you just had to have, no matter what it cost. And, said Tombo,

139

there was the old storeroom which had become a distribution centre for the country-wide trade.

'Big money,' said Tombo again. 'And behind it there's somebody a whole lot bigger than Harry Decker. You got to hit them fast, before they get their next consignment out on the streets.'

'You're sure there's one due in?'

'I might be wrong, but – '

'Come on, Tombo. You know. I can tell you do.'

'The way I heard it, a big delivery tomorrow morning. Late morning. Then they start sorting and packaging. You know. Could take some time.'

'What time do *you* reckon would be good for a visit?'

Tombo slumped down on the bench. 'It'll take careful planning.'

'What time, Tombo?'

'Hit it at half three. Tomorrow afternoon. That way they should be right in the middle of it.'

'Fine.' Galloway turned, and at last Tombo faced him, apprehensive. 'I'll need you in there, though.'

'That's what I've been dreading you'd say. Look, they'll kill me if they ever find out – and that, my white brother, is not a figure of speech!'

'All you have to do,' said Galloway soothingly, 'is be in there when we hit the place. You'll be my eyes and ears. Just point me in the right direction, the right places to look, and the right people to nick. No more.'

'Will I be arrested?'

'Of course. Got to make it look convincing, haven't we?'

'Then what?'

'Well, my old son,' Galloway smiled, 'have you ever heard the story about the one that gets away?'

He was impatient to get moving now. Everything had to be set up fast, but just right. He hurried downstairs to a pay-phone outside the stadium's changing rooms, and fretted while the bleeps went on and on for ever – did they have a siesta every day now at Sun Hill? – until he was through to Ted Roach.

The briefing was set up. Things to be said and done shuffled themselves and reshuffled in his head.

'And don't tell anybody *anything*,' he concluded.

'What're you talking about, guv?' came Roach's plaintive response. 'I don't *know* anything.'

They would all know soon enough.

The campaign began to take shape. In Roy Galloway's mind, for a start. He could visualize the dilapidated old cinema, looking so scruffy and abandoned from outside, but within those boards and padlocked doors so full of life – and the potential for death and drug-sodden despair.

He couldn't wait to get in there.

Ted Roach had been on early turn and ought to have left by the time Galloway got back. But he was hanging about, fidgeting, gnawing at a wisp of his moustache, dying to know what the hell this was all about.

'Who's on tonight?' Galloway demanded.

'I am,' said Dashwood.

Roach had to agree. 'He is.'

'Right, you can go, Ted.'

'Not if I'm going to miss anything, I'm not.'

'Haven't you got somebody waiting back there to offer you some health-giving crackling?'

'I don't mind hanging on, honest, guv.'

'Okay. There are some calls that have to be made. Share 'em out between you. Oh – and did you fix for the super to come back in?'

Roach grinned evilly. 'Like you said. And the way he reacted, I'd say you'd better come up with something hot.'

'I aim to do just that.'

'Tell you what, guv. Why not see him first, and cover for – '

'I'm not covering for anything or anybody. Not for more hours than I have to, any road. We get organized right here
141

and now, and then you've got something to occupy your little minds while I go and spell it out for him.'

'It really is that hot?' Roach knew when the joking was over and the real thing was on its way.

'Scorch the pants off you. Right. This is what I want on standby for tomorrow.' He paused for a moment while Dashwood grabbed a scrap pad from his desk. 'All right? A couple of drugs dogs, but I don't want anyone else told about that for the time being. Two nondescript vans, one with ladders. The ladders are to be used, not for show. About ten lads from the crime squad – no, make that twenty. And remember, don't mention to them about the drugs dogs. Not until I say so. Some lamps, sledgehammers . . . yeah, I think that's about all for now.'

'Blimey.' Even Ted Roach was awestruck. 'What we gonna hit – Fort Knox?'

'Get it moving.' Galloway watched them both diving for their phones before he went up to face Chief Superintendent Brownlow.

Next morning, with encouragement and warnings ringing in both ears, like a stereo music centre gone on the blink, he was at the magistrates' court in the motley pile-up waiting for cases to be called, under the beady eye of a uniformed sergeant on a high stool, bolstered up by the legal power invested in him.

WPC Ackland, he noticed, was standing below the desk as Galloway entered. The jailer was saying: 'There's a warrant outstanding on Mrs Drew. Non-payment of fine. I've told the clerk.'

Maggie, close beside June Ackland, bridled. Ackland looked cross. 'The CRO didn't say anything about that.'

'Breakdown of communications. You know how it is.'

Galloway said: 'Looking for a couple of cheap tins of salmon, Bert?'

'Wouldn't get anything cheap off me, I can tell yer,' cried Maggie, uncharacteristically ferocious.

Galloway sidled closer to June Ackland. 'You got the

message about the plain clothes this afternoon? Old jeans, scruffy old sweater, that kind of thing.'

Her brown eyes began to burn. 'Really something this time, sir?'

'Oh, really something. Wouldn't say no to a bulletproof bra, if I were you.' He glanced up at the lordly jailer. 'Who's on the bench?'

'Redmayne.'

Galloway allowed himself a happy click of the fingers. There wasn't going to be any legalistic needling and niggling, not with Redmayne. He slid unobtrusively into Court Number One.

'What I intend to do,' the magistrate was intoning, 'is to put this case back to later in the day, so that you may have a meaningful talk with the probation officer. This does not necessarily mean I'm going to place you on probation. Thank you. You may step down.'

Just as the clerk of the court was about to announce the next case, the court officer hastened forward. 'Would you take an application for a search warrant, sir? Inspector Galloway.'

From here on it all had to roll at top speed. One delay, one word out of place, one rumour snaking its well-oiled way round the grapevine, and the whole thing could fall apart. Galloway held himself ready, and felt a few beads of sweat prickle on the back of his neck and start leaking downwards. There was a nod of acceptance. He took the warrant and information forms from his inside pocket and handed them to the usher, who handed them to the clerk of the court. A polite gesture of the hand, and he was in the witness box with the card in front of him, taking the oath, declaring his name and official position, agreeing that his signature was in fact his signature, and testifying that the information he had offered was true to the best of his knowledge and belief.

It had happened so many times before. But this time it was somehow ten times more important. Those scum had to be done down. That housing estate had to be shielded from

143

drugs and the drug peddlers and all the high-placed, high-priced bastards who made fortunes out of human misery.

This was when being a copper actually meant something. It was why you'd joined, why you'd slogged on, and why it had to be made to work.

One false step, one snag, and it was all blown.

The magistrate read quickly over the depositions, signed, and reached for the official stamp. At the last moment he seemed to have second thoughts. Galloway held his breath. Redmayne, the magistrate, tore off a small scrap of paper, scribbled on it, and attached it with a paper clip to the rest. Then he leaned forward and passed the warrant over.

Galloway quickened his pace round the edge of the court, not looking at the note until he was close to the door.

The brief scrawl said: 'Best of luck.'

Galloway paused and offered a grateful smile. The magistrate did not exactly smile in return, but over the edge of his bi-focals his eyebrows rose in what could only have been a semaphore of encouragement.

It was a good omen. Roy Galloway began to feel the adrenalin reaching parts other stimulants usually failed to reach.

Fifteen

Final briefing in the parade room was low key, yet as fraught with the awareness of danger as a wartime invasion briefing. Although they all knew the target building, squatting as it did in the middle of a run-down street with side alleys from which they regularly winkled out glue-sniffers and meths drinkers, only a few of them had ever been inside it. The lettering of its one-time name had cracked and distorted long ago, and three-ply boards masked spaces where posters had once invited audiences to queue for the latest all-star features. Harry Decker had never replaced the sign with anything to identify his illegal drinking club, but some longer-serving officers could remember visiting it nevertheless. They were the ones with key duties today.

Uniformed men mingled with men and women in a motley array of plain clothes, grabbing chairs where they could or leaning against the back wall of the room with a clear view of the blackboard. Galloway had gone over the route and the division of the attacking forces three times, word for word, as if afraid to reach zero hour and let them loose.

Chief Superintendent Brownlow broke in at last. 'Right, I think that's it. You all know what to do. I don't have to reiterate the importance of this raid. If it's successful, it'll be a significant step forward in our fight against drug abuse. Unfortunately, this in turn will attract considerable publicity. Therefore I must impress on you that I don't want any cock-ups. Whether we win or lose, I want no cause for complaint. I want this operation carried out properly. And let me remind you . . . if there are no drugs found, then there are no drugs found. Understood? Rules and regulations, right on the line.'

He stood aside, leaving room for Roy Galloway to come forward again. 'Anything else you'd like to add?'

'Only what I've said before. When you go in, speed is the essence. As soon as we turn into that back street, make no mistake, the word'll be out. So when I give the off, don't hesitate – *go!*'

They all looked at the wall clock. That was all they wanted now – just to go.

'Ted, your group has got to get up those back stairs fast. You remember where they start, right inside the emergency door?'

'I remember, guv. Don't worry about us.'

'Sergeant Penny, steer your lot away from the edge of the circle. It may look a quick way from one side to the other, but some nasty person might chuck one or two of you over the edge. Right. Those of you with sledge-hammers, crowbars and the rest of it – don't leave them behind in the rush from wherever you're staked out. I don't want any last-minute problems getting into the place.'

'The lamps,' said Brownlow. 'I think you should mention them.'

'Yes, sir. Thanks. The lamps.' Galloway waved Sergeant Cryer forward. 'Sergeant Cryer is one of the few people who personally knows the layout of Decker's. He's been on two previous raids. Listen carefully.'

Bob Cryer said: 'As soon as they know we're hitting the place, the first thing they'll do is switch off the electricity at the mains. Now when that happens, whatever you're doing you'll stay put until those of you with lamps switch them on. Remember, there are no windows in those corridors. It'll be as black as hell. We don't want to be held up by any accidents or to start belting one another. It'll be my job to get those lights on again as soon as possible. But while I'm at it, the rest of you make sure each group's got a lamp with them.'

'Any other questions?' There was a reedy dryness in Galloway's throat.

One of the uniformed constables said: 'You mentioned an inside man. How will we recognize him?'

'You won't. I don't want this person to receive any special treatment. Could be more than his life's worth. So it's better that you don't know his or her identity.' His eyes narrowed. 'Right then, that's it. See you on the plot.'

'And good luck to all of you,' said Brownlow.

They moved out.

It was a quiet afternoon, and all the quieter on the approaches to the cinema. This end of the manor had declined since the modern High Street shopping precinct was developed. Little shops which had once been as bright and busy as the cinema were shabby and, in several cases, gapingly empty. A few coloured boys sprawled on a doorstep. A road sweeper pushing his broom down the gutter from the main road along the side street was muttering under his breath as he made his way round a builder's lorry parked on double yellow lines. At the entrance to Decker's premises the two minders yawned and gazed unsuspiciously along the pavement. The black one, Ritt, was Tombo Robinson's old crony; Pat Corcoran, the mean-faced white, managed to look vicious even when he was bored.

A red van turned in from the main road, slowing as it drew closer to the parked lorry with its cargo of builders' ladders. It looked as if the driver was going to jump down and have an argument with the man blocking his way.

He did jump down. So, like shapes released from a sud- denly exploding firework, did a dozen others. They burst out of the back of the van, two of them with dogs bounding across the pavement, others dragging the ladders into the road and swinging them up against the side wall of the cinema. The roadsweeper chucked his broom expertly into his little wheeled cart and snatched up a sledge-hammer. The ends of the streets were swiftly blocked off by a Panda car and a transit van.

Ritt let out a yell and turned to the dangling padlock on the door. Ted Roach went for him head down, and carried

147

him hard against the wall. Corcoran ducked, wrenched the padlock aside, and went in, trying to kick the door shut behind him. They heard the rattle of a bar falling across it from inside.

Dashwood was halfway across the street with a sledge-hammer, wielding it like a battle-axe as he attacked the door. A great gash was torn down one panel. Then another, and another.

At the same time two plain-clothes men were shinning up a ladder propped under a small back window which Ted Roach had identified as the most likely one for entry to the passage by the projection room. Jimmy Carver and Taffy Edwards were halfway up the fire escape, making for the roof. WPCs Ackland and Martela were waved back by Gallo-way: they were too eager to hurl themselves inside the moment the doors collapsed. Their turn would come, when the drug-sodden women inside began to realize what was going on.

There was a satisfying, splintering crash. The bigger of the two doors was down. Galloway and Cryer went over the debris, leading the assault wave like troops going over the top of a trench.

The doors of the upstairs foyer must have swung open as Corcoran reached them. Above a murmur of music they heard his yell:

'The fuzz!'

Galloway and a uniformed constable pounded up the stairs, while Cryer hurried off along a side passage. The double doors to the foyer were still scraping together as Galloway flung himself at them. Then a chair leg was thrust towards the round glass windows, and slotted between the handles. Inside, people had been dancing drowsily in the crimson-lit foyer, but were now pulling apart. A man at the bar was bundling something into a suitcase.

'Get one of those hammers up here!'

Dashwood lumbered up behind him.

148

Inside, Decker was shouting: 'The lights, Pat – go and knock the lights off!'

Dashwood swung the sledge-hammer. His face glowed in the lurid light through the glass windows. He looked as if he was enjoying himself.

The doors shook. He braced himself, tried again. The second time glass shattered and tinkled about his feet. The third time, the improvised bolt cracked and the doors began to sag.

Then the lights went out.

At once a lamp went on behind Galloway and Dashwood.

There was no way that even the most skilled tactician could control events now. You couldn't be everywhere at once. It was every man for himself – just as it was for Decker and his pals. Galloway prayed that every separate group, every man and woman inside the building and outside, was functioning the way it had been laid down in advance.

Carver and Edwards ought to be on the roof, mopping up any fly character who knew of an escape route that way. Bob Cryer ought to be somewhere near the main switches by now – the nearer and sooner, the better. Junkies summoning up the energy to make a dash for it through the old front doors should be falling obligingly into the hands of two uniformed sergeants, Dave Litten and PC Smith.

While he himself and the wildly energetic, destructive Dashwood . . .

Galloway flung his shoulder against the doors, and was through. The beam of the powerful torch followed him, probing across the floor as phantom shapes scurried away through the far doors. A couple of abandoned knives shone in the stab of light. Three or four syringes had been dropped in the panic. And there was one man lying face down, near the door, with something dark shadowing his back and left hip.

The light picked him out and stayed on him, catching a glint from the bloodstained flick-knife a few inches away.

149

Galloway went down on his knees and carefully turned the man's head.

It was Tombo Robinson. His lips moved, and for a second it seemed that his eyes had tried to open. But that might have been a trick of the light.

'Somebody get an ambulance!'

All at once the lights came on again. The mess strewn across the floor looked even worse. Tombo Robinson made a pleading, whining sound in his throat.

Corcoran and Harry Decker were halfway down the arc of the stairs when the lights glowed into life above them and below. Sergeant Penny and a constable stood by the bottom step, waiting. When they turned, Ted Roach and Dashwood were framed in the shattered doors of the upper foyer.

The dog-handlers came in, moving purposefully from one littered room to another, sniffing out a small trap-door behind the bar, growling gently as helpless groups of sagging, doped men and women were shepherded past them and settled on the edge of the desolate cinema balcony.

Bob Cryer reappeared at Galloway's side.

'Recognize any of 'em?' Galloway waved at the sullen faces and bowed heads.

'Not in this bloody light. Talk about psychedelic!'

'Decker's not amongst them. Or that other gorilla of his. Any news from downstairs?'

'Still sorting them out, but it didn't look like it. Could have slipped the net.'

'Shouldn't have. Not the way we've got this place sewn up. He'll be about here somewhere.'

'And what's this I hear about someone getting stabbed?'

The adrenalin which had driven Galloway at top speed through this last twenty minutes wasn't racing any more. He said dully: 'Still breathing, luckily.'

'Inside man, Roy?'

He could not bring himself to answer.

Feet shuffled closer. Sergeant Penny and one of his men were wheeling a couple of men in to join the others.

Bob Cryer breathed a sigh of congratulation. 'Like you said, Roy. About here somewhere.'

'Guv!' One of the dog-handlers was waving from a corner. 'Come and see this.'

It was a nice, neat little cache, tidily wrapped up and tidily awaiting collection. Galloway watched it being lifted out, and turned back to confront Harry Decker.

'Come on over here, you. Hold his hand, sergeant. Let him at least see what he's going to be nicked for.'

'Whatever it is, it's nothing to do with me. I've never seen it before.'

It was a relief, at last, to be able to laugh. A great laugh, not just at Harry Decker and Harry Decker's chances of getting away with that, but at the whole operation – a gusty laugh of achievement, triumph, sheer exuberance.

Behind the laughter, for Galloway, was the dark thought of Tombo Robinson.

He plodded down the stairs to supervise the loading of their prisoners and wrap up the last little detail. By now the streets outside looked a whole lot livelier, not just with police and captives but with curious onlookers who had crept out of the woodwork.

Sergeant Penny took charge of the invaluable suitcases. Both as goods and as evidence they formed a rich haul. Thousands of pounds worth of 'smack', and all of it a great weight on the shoulders of Decker and whoever his accomplices were. That would take some sorting out, but sorted out it was going to be.

Galloway watched an ambulance driving away.

If only . . .

June Ackland came hurrying along the pavement. 'Sir!'

'Later, love. Right now – '

'It's important, sir. Carver and Edwards have just been on the air. They chased a man who came out on the roof. He got over to that car park over the way. Tried to run them down in a car.'

'Did he get away?'

151

'Yes.'

'Stupid buggers.'

The radio crackled incessantly and argumentatively from the Panda car. A police transit van edged past it, and doors were thrown open. Prisoners were marshalled into it. Roach and Dashwood emerged into the open air and joined Galloway, looking pleased with themselves and yet a bit sorry that the short burst of excitement and violence was ended. You didn't often get such a chance to flex your muscles.

'Those weapons and things,' rapped Galloway. 'All that junk on the floor of the foyer. I want the whole lot photographed *in situ*, right? Mike, you can help the SOCO to package. I know it'll take a long time, but it's got to be done properly.'

'Right.'

'Ted' – this was the routine wrap-up, after all the punch-ups – 'you're to start questioning everyone up there. And what I want is a witness to the stabbing. Rules and regulations, remember. All according to the book. But somebody must have seen something.' He watched them set off back into the building, and turned his attention to June Ackland. 'That car – did they get the number?'

'Yes, sir.'

'That's something, anyway. Has it been circulated?'

'No.'

This was too much. 'Then *get* it circulated.'

'Sir . . . it's got CD plates on it!' _Diplomatic_

The corridor outside the charge room was milling with people like commuters at Charing Cross station learning that drivers had just started a work-to-rule. Doggedly Chief Superintendent Brownlow elbowed his way against the tide, fighting a way out to the freedom of the yard just as another van drew in and disgorged its dazed, dismal occupants. Quite a haul, it had to be admitted. This time a lot of the charges were going to stick. It was a warming thought. Maybe now the Clayview estate tenants would feel a bit warmer towards Sun Hill, too.

Roy Galloway ran a hand through his ruffled hair, tacky with sweat, and said: 'Sir. Glad to see you. I was just coming up to have a word with you. We've got trouble – a very interesting development.'

Behind him the Panda car reversed, tacked, and shot off again to collect more chunks of evidence.

'I know,' said Brownlow tightly. 'I've had two national dailies on the phone already, telling me I've had a raid. One insists I've recovered half a million's worth of heroin, and the other that a man's been stabbed. And both of them want to know if it's true an embassy car was involved.'

'Bloody hell. How did they find that out?'

'I don't know.' Brownlow's voice was drowned by the tumult as a transit van jolted to a halt and another load of prisoners came out, mumbling and swearing and shouting. 'Look, I think we'd better go up to my office. You'd better put me in the picture before the commissioner rings.'

The office was quieter, but there was still an intermittent throb from downstairs as doors opened and shut, and men and women were herded in from the yard to be questioned and, when the paperwork was completed, charged.

After the uproar of smashed doors and the chatter of excited radios and the complaints of junkies and the heavies who had found they were not as heavy as they had thought, this silence was not soothing. Roy Galloway, at any rate, did not find it soothing. He listened, pretending not to listen, while Brownlow put in three phone calls and made polite acknowledgements and sat back, having done everything according to the book; then, unable to stay still after all that had happened, he loosened his tie and began to pace up and down.

'Roy, for heavens' sake! We can't do a thing until Special Branch ring back.'

How long did it take Special Branch, then, to check on an embassy car? Galloway himself could have extracted the information they needed in seconds from the computer. But of course that was not the way hard-headed old diplomatic wheeler-dealers organized things way up there in their own protected stratosphere. Any minute now there might well be a sly hint that Carver and Edwards had imagined a Mercedes and a number-plate just because they had lost their man and needed a get-out. This was becoming a different ball game. Systems were laid down, and when it came to embassy cars you abided by a different code of instructions. Facts went out of the window: protocol was what counted, diplomatic bureaucracy was what called the tune. Galloway's stomach knotted up. They had come so close to cracking one of the biggest drug operations so far seen in this area, but instead of concentrating every last effort on the material right there in their hands they were hanging about on the end of a telephone at the whim of some pussyfooting civil servant.

Brownlow said: 'I know how frustrated you must feel, Roy, but it's out of our hands. What worries me more than anything at the moment, and should be worrying you, is Tombo Robinson.'

'He'll be all right. People like Tombo always survive.'

'What if he claims compensation? Have you thought about that? I was against involving outsiders right from the beginning, remember?'

Clearly Roy Galloway was not going to be allowed to forget. Brownlow, like everybody else in this racket, was armouring himself against any conceivable repercussion.

The phone rang. Galloway tensed. Brownlow answered, then held out the receiver.

Ted Roach said: 'I've got a witness, guv. That's the good news. He says the man we're looking for is a well-dressed feller. That ties in with what Taffy Edwards saw. He's the supplier, the top man. Very smart indeed. Just the type you'd expect to have a smart suitcase and an embassy car. And on top of that, he saw how that black got knifed – trying to get one of the doors unbarred so we could get in. Stabbed by that scum Corcoran.' There was the slightest hesitation, then: 'Your inside man, guv?'

154

'If that's the good news,' rasped Galloway, 'then what the hell's the bad news?'

'He won't give evidence. It's an "in confidence" deal.'

'Oh, the hell it is. Can't you put some pressure on him to give evidence?' He caught Chief Superintendent Brownlow's disapproving glare. 'All right, softly softly, if that's how it has to be. But keep at him. And listen, Ted . . .'

As he was talking, the other phone on the desk rang. Brownlow murmured into it, sat upright, and reached for a notepad. After a moment he scrawled a name and turned the pad towards Galloway. The name was that of Simbula. Could mean anything, so far as Roy Galloway was concerned. He shook his head. When both of them had put their receivers down, Brownlow said:

'Simbula. A West African state. Very important right now – and very, very delicate.'

'Delicate?' Galloway exploded. 'Look, we've got a description of the car, we've got its number, we've got a pretty good description of the man from both Carver and Edwards, and by God I'll promise that we'll screw confirmation out of that witness Ted's got with him right now – '

'No description. Not the man, not the car. I told you, it's a very delicate situation. My instructions are to sit tight until someone from the Home Office rings.'

'The Home Office? And then maybe the Foreign Office. And then God knows what creepy little erk who's being paid to fiddle the public relations image of some tinpot African state that happens to be in favour this week! Well, I'm not hanging around here waiting. Ted's hauling in that prisoner and I'm going to question him about the stabbing, and I'm just in the mood to do it.'

Before he could reach the door, the chief superintendent was commandingly on his feet. 'No, Roy. I'm not having you questioning anybody until you've cooled down. That's an order.'

'Then what am I supposed to do? Sit down and twiddle my thumbs?'

'What I would suggest, Roy, is that you go to the hospital and check on Robinson. That'll give you time to simmer down a little. By the time you get back we should be in a better position to know what steps to take in this matter.'

It was by no means a suggestion. Like the earlier bit, it was an order. Roy Galloway had to accept it, admitting it made sense. Somebody else had taken the responsibility, and he ought to be grateful for that. But he would sooner have taken the responsibility for everything and done it his own way. That way they might quite possibly have come out of this carve-up with some truth and justice. As if that had anything to do with it. Some Whitehall mandarin, he knew in his bones, was already making the real decisions.

He went down to the car and revved up with a loud snarl which was nowhere near as loud as he would have liked to make it.

A fussy little Greek car park attendant at the hospital screamed at him that he was not a doctor, he couldn't leave his car here, it would be towed away, he was to go off, go off now, get off these premises. Galloway shoved his warrant card close enough to the man's face to scratch his nose and make his eyes water, and trod on into the hospital.

Young PC Lewis was chatting to a girl behind a sliding glass window by the reception area. He made an attempt at standing to attention as Galloway approached.

'All right, son. What's happening?'

'He's in the operating theatre. Or was fifteen minutes ago.'

'Any news?'

'From what I can gather, internal bleeding. I don't know any more than that. Oh, except one thing, sir.'

'Yes?'

'His correct name. He gave a false name at first, but the doctor soon sorted him out. It's Robinson. Lives on the Clayview estate.'

Galloway tried to stop a muscle in his cheek twitching. 'Robinson, eh?' he said indifferently.

PC Lewis nodded past him. 'That's the doctor, sir. Coming through those swing doors.'

Galloway watched a rather scrawny, youngish middle-aged woman in a white coat let the doors swing shut behind her as she headed for a hot drinks dispenser. Her hand trembled as she touched the dispenser, stared unseeingly at it for a moment, then groped in her pocket for change.

'Her name's Bison,' Lewis supplied.

Galloway walked across and produced a fifty-pence piece.

'Doctor Bison, isn't it? I'm Inspector Galloway. Sun Hill police station. Coffee?'

'Thank you, inspector.'

He waited until the coffee had poured steaming into the cup, then took a deep breath. 'About . . . Robinson.'

'We lost him, I'm afraid.'

'Lost him?'

'He's dead,' she said, with a sort of pent-up inner fury. 'Nothing we could do. There were complications.'

'Nothing you could do,' said Galloway dully.

'We could have saved him in normal circumstances, but his inside was in such a state. His liver was inflamed, completely out of all proportion – an advanced form of serum hepatitis.'

'Hepatitis?' he echoed.

'It's a common disease amongst drug addicts. Usually transmitted by means of a contaminated syringe needle.'

'An addict?' Galloway fought to get it into perspective, and lost. This was the craziest thing of the whole grubby story. 'Robinson an addict?'

'A registered drug addict for some years.' The doctor's face was lean and sadly philosophical. To her, Tombo Robinson was just another case history, a sad and frustrating, lamentable but all too common slab of medical history. 'He was weaned off heroin,' she explained, 'to methadone and other substances. Then, like many others, he went back to heroin. The clinic dealing with him lost contact about . . . oh, somewhere around twelve months ago. Which usually means he was back to buying it on the streets. If we'd had his records available from the beginning we might just have saved him, but for some reason he started out giving a false name.' She waited for Galloway to make some comment. When he remained silent, choking down something sour and terrifying inside himself, she said: 'Will you be informing the next of kin?'

Galloway turned automatically towards the exit.

'Inspector . . . ?'

Near the door, PC Lewis stepped hurriedly forward. 'Sir, will I be relieved for grub?'

Galloway went down the steps towards his car.

In the passage outside the charge room, June Ackland patted her hair into some sort of order and said: 'Phew, I just want a shower. Just the thought of it! That place was absolutely filthy.'

'Sorry, love, you'll have to stick it out for a while.' Bob Cryer turned as Galloway came in and headed for the stairs. 'Oh, Roy, come and count the . . .'.

Galloway went on his way. When he reached the chief superintendent's office he stormed in without knocking, to find himself faced not only by Brownlow but by two visitors, comfortably settled on chairs which must have been commandeered from another room. They were all holding whisky glasses, glowing amber in the light from the window.

'Ah, Roy.' Brownlow got up, lowering his right eyebrow in a warning frown. 'Do come in. Shut the door.'

Galloway shut the door and stood where he was, sizing up the two other men. One of them was an easily identifiable Whitehall product in a dark blue, pin-striped suit with an old school tie which Galloway did not recognize – not that it had ever been one of his hobbies to recognize old school ties.

'Let me introduce Mr North,' said Brownlow, 'from the Home Office.'

North favoured the detective inspector with an aloof nod, clearly categorizing him without hesitation and deciding just what helping of cool politeness to offer.

'And Mr Gilmoco,' said Brownlow, 'of the Simbulan embassy.'

Gilmoco was a smooth, almost glossy black. He had a rather noble hooked nose, lips which seemed ready to express amusement at the slightest provocation, and shrewdly watchful eyes. Unlike North, he half rose to his feet and held out his hand. The cuffs of a smart grey suit and matching shirt fell back from a gold bracelet as he did so.

Galloway ignored the gesture. Hastily the chief super waved him to a hard-backed chair beside the desk and dived into a bottom drawer for another glass. His eyes silently ordered Galloway to behave himself, play it cool.

He said: 'Mr Gilmoco has kindly furnished us with just the information we need to crack this case. We now have the full picture, Roy, and it's quite an interesting one.' He poured a generous measure of Scotch and pushed the glass towards the edge of the desk. 'I think you'll be pleased.'

You'd better be, said his gaze.

'Perhaps it would be more expedient if Mr Gilmoco explained to the inspector,' said North, almost deferential as he turned to offer the diplomat his cue.

'Thank you.' Gilmoco smiled agreeably at North and then, without any change of intensity, at Galloway. 'It's a matter of one of our embassy officials, inspector. A junior official, I might add.'

'Who will remain nameless,' offered North smoothly.

'Quite so. He has in fact been under close scrutiny for some time. We have not been happy, I assure you. He was suspected of bringing large quantities of heroin into Britain through the diplomatic bag. We could not be sure – these things are awkward and often very distressing – and his motive at first was not known and rather puzzling. Therefore – '

'There were sinister connotations, inspector,' North cut in. 'Security was of course the embassy's prime concern. And still is!'

'We thought it prudent to allow him to continue, so that

159

we had a clear understanding . . . er . . .' He had allowed himself to look straight at Galloway, and Galloway's stare threw him for a moment.

'Inspector Galloway fully appreciates the position you were in,' said Brownlow quickly.

'Perhaps you should get straight to the point, Mr Gilmoco.' You had to hand it to Whitehall: when moral support was needed, they could hand it out – but not always to the most moral types.

'Our man, inspector, was being blackmailed by a Mr Gavin. Some indiscretion concerning a young boy. The price for Gavin's silence was smuggling heroin into Britain.'

'How long have you known about the blackmail?' asked Galloway stonily.

'Only since the Foreign Office informed us our embassy car was involved in the incident. We did not waste time, inspector, you must grant us that. We immediately questioned the official concerned. He spoke with candour about his part in the affair.'

Galloway wondered how much that candour owed to remorse and how much to whatever methods they were accustomed to use within the embassy walls.

'I've already checked on Gavin, Roy,' contributed Brownlow. 'He's been involved in blackmail before, and the Drug Squad at the Yard has quite a file on him.'

'My official tells me the arrangement was always the same. He would put the suitcase of heroin into the embassy car and drive it to a rendezvous. Usually it was a public car park. Gavin would then use the embassy car to make his deliveries . . .'

So the story rolled on. Galloway registered every word yet was somehow not really hearing the thing all in one piece. Because there wasn't one whole piece. None of it bore any relation to what he knew in every fibre of his being to be the truth. But here was a well-dressed, well-educated Englishman obsequiously nodding at every one of Gilmoco's excuses, and Brownlow watching not Gilmoco but his own detective inspector, not wanting anything so embarrassing as talk about the truth.

Brownlow knew. Oh, Brownlow knew all right. But he was not going to say anything. You got promotion faster by not saying things than by saying them; and you kept where you were by keeping a civil tongue in your head, not asking too many questions – except when it came to asking questions of people who hadn't the power to slap you down. These two smoothies had the power, all right.

'Who'd think of stopping a car with CD plates?' said Brownlow.

'Precisely,' said North.

Galloway pushed the whisky glass away. 'Why are you telling me all this?'

'So that you will understand.'

'Understand what?'

'That the embassy official will be claiming diplomatic immunity,' said North. 'But he will be recalled.'

'And go free?'

'Roy!' said Brownlow warningly.

Gilmoco leaned forward, still playing the diplomatic line and exuding goodwill. 'No. He will be severely punished on his return to Simbula. This I can promise you, inspector.'

North cleared his throat and folded his arms across his chest to show that he regarded this as a good moment to close the discussion. Everything had been explained, so far as the Home Office was concerned. Everything had been done for the best.

'Inspector Galloway, Mr Gilmoco has gone out of his way to give you this information. It shows a co-operation between our two countries to stamp out the illegal traffic in heroin. Simbula does not wish to become a point in a new Golden Triangle.'

'It sounds nice and tidy. And what about Gavin?'

'That is surely a concern for our own authorities, not Simbula. Mr Brownlow tells me you have what I believe is called an "inside man". I don't have to tell you your job,

161

inspector, but surely if this man is as good as Mr Brownlow says then he'll have no trouble infiltrating any new drugs ring Gavin may set up.'

'My inside man, eh? You think it'll be that easy?'

'I'm sure a substantial reward would be an incentive, don't you? Something could be arranged. Those sort of people – '

'Those sort of people!' Roy Galloway crashed to his feet. 'Let me tell you – '

'No, Roy!'

'I'm sorry, guv. I know I'm out of order, but there's some things have got to be said.' He pointed past North and Gilmoco towards the window. Automatically their heads turned. 'Out there,' raged Galloway, 'I've got parents at their wits' end, pouring their hearts out to me. Wanting to know what I'm doing, what any of us are doing, about heroin flooding on to their estate. Killing their kids. *Killing* them! And I have to listen to you talking about this job as if it's simply an embarrassment to some foreign embassy. Gentlemen, I've got an epidemic out there.'

North said: 'Let me assure you – '

'You can't assure me of anything, Mr North. You should be representing us . . . making the kinds of noise I'm making, not sitting there wet-nursing Mr Gilmoco. This is a Home Office problem and nothing to do with any foreign embassy. The problem is here at home, on this patch. And anyone who brings that muck on to this patch ought to be jumped on. Hard. Not shipped back home with a little slap on the wrist.'

'Inspector' – North's manner was getting a bit ragged round the edges – 'my department is deeply concerned about heroin abuse. There is in fact, at this very moment, a Home Office working party considering this tragic problem. But this particular matter is something entirely different. There are underlying complications which I cannot go into. Matters of which I cannot speak. I was hoping you would understand, Mr Galloway.'

'Oh, I understand all right. Only you try explaining to those parents out there. See if *they* understand!'

'I think you've said enough, Roy.' Brownlow had given up trying to control the situation by warning glances. 'You've made your point,' he said firmly and finally.

It was no good. Galloway was going to say it once and for all. 'A few moments ago, Mr North, you tried to tell me how to do my job. Well, let me tell you I'll crack this case with or without your help or the embassy's help. I'll have the evidence to convict Gavin. It may take more time than I would like, but I'll get there.' He stormed to the door. 'Oh, and by the way. My "inside man", for your information, was one of those parents. He's dead.'

It was like lashing a whip across Brownlow's face. All right, let him feel it.

'Dead,' Galloway repeated. 'Trying to help us pull off this job. But then you wouldn't understand that, would you? Good day, gentlemen.'

He slammed the door behind him, and left them to it.

Sixteen

Carver and Edwards had got there first, and hard on their heels was Sergeant Cryer. Dave Litten could see that DI Galloway was not best chuffed with this. They had driven at one hell of a lick through the streets, in a manner which did not increase Litten's respect for Galloway's driving, and at the end of it all the uniformed boys were there ahead of them. Litten tried to look as if he had worn plain clothes on the job for most of his career so far. Of course for the time being he was only on secondment, but the formalities would soon be over. He was at the detective inspector's side now, ready for anything, and that was how he was going to stay.

Not that he approved of Galloway's motives in rushing to the scene of the crime. Just because a real live lord was involved, did everybody from Sun Hill have to drop everything and run along to make respectful noises?

It looked like it. As they skidded to a halt there were already two cars at the kerb with their lights flashing, striking reflections from the brass knocker on the small but fashionably tarted-up Victorian terraced house. There were blue flowers in the window-boxes, and blue uniforms indoors.

PC Carver came down the steps as Galloway started up them. 'Where are you off to, lad, hey?'

'Doing a door to door, sir.'

'Better move your arse then, hadn't you?'

Jimmy Carver made a face at Dave Litten as he passed. 'What's wrong with him?'

Remembering the pork pie abandoned on the pub counter after the phone had rung, Litten grinned. 'Indigestion.

164

Always the same after he's had a big meal.' He trotted loyally up the steps after his master.

The hallway retained traces of its nineteenth-century origin, some of them deliberately emphasized: the hatstand must have been bought somewhere along the King's Road, and although the florid wallpaper had the authentic atmosphere it was obviously new. But the combined bedroom and studio which occupied a large part of the first floor was a fine old mix of the impulses of its present owner.

He was tall and limp, with an inherited aristocratic face above scruffy denims. On the huge brass bedstead dominating the room was a girl with her knees drawn up under her chin, combining the waiflike charm of a little girl hardly out of her teens with the glazed expression of someone who had lived several decades too long and wondered when she would be allowed to pack up and have a long sleep.

Sergeant Cryer was saying: 'You can be sure, your lordship, that everything possible is . . . Ah.' He turned with a wickedly welcoming smile. 'Here is Inspector Galloway himself.'

Litten observed Galloway's shoulders stiffen and his chin go up as he paced to the centre of the room.

'Inspector Galloway . . . Lord Barstow-Smythe.' Bob Cryer made the introduction with a caricature of a bow.

Lord Barstow-Smythe was not interested in formalities. 'How long will it take you to recover my jewellery, inspector?' His voice had a dying fall to it, sad and weary – but ready to become spiteful and complaining.

Caught unawares, Galloway glanced desperately at Cryer, who obliged. 'His lordship's necklace in particular, inspector. I told his lordship you've already got things moving.'

'Quite right.' Galloway improvised with growing assurance. 'The moment we heard, we circulated the basic information throughout the Metropolitan Police district. And' – he turned to Dave Litten, who virtually sprang to attention – 'Constable Litten here has alerted Interpol.'

Litten nodded efficiently.

'It's not the money that matters. It's just that one particular

165

piece of jewellery – sentimental value more than anything else. It was presented to the family by Her Royal Highness the – '

'A photograph?' Galloway cut in. 'And an insurance description of the items, anything like that?'

The girl slowly lifted her chin as if to contribute to the conversation. Then with infinite slowness she shifted into a cross-legged position but offered no other helpful response.

'Now you've mentioned it, inspector' – Barstow-Smythe appeared to have as much trouble as the girl in getting to grips with reality – 'it was all valued, not twelve months ago, at Sotheby's. And a photograph? Yes, I might . . . excuse me a moment, gentlemen, while I pop downstairs.'

In his absence Cryer and Galloway examined the room. Somebody had certainly turned it over, but without making the disgusting mess a lot of them went in for. There were some rooms you never wanted to live in again after they'd fouled them. This room, thought Dave Litten, wasn't one he'd have wanted to live in in the first place, but apart from a few drawers ripped out and a glass bottle on the dressing-table smashed, it hadn't suffered a lot.

'Litten!'

'Sir?'

'Don't just stand there. Check downstairs, find out if there've been any callers. When PC Carver comes back, see if anyone's reported a frequent visitor, anyone sniffing around. And I noticed when I came in that there's a nosey cow on the first floor opposite. If anything's happened in this street she'd have seen it, you can bet your life.'

Cryer winked. 'You don't miss a trick, Roy.'

'That's what it's all about, sarge.'

They skirted the bed, glancing covertly at the girl in the middle of it. You definitely wouldn't have risked having *her* valued at Sotheby's.

It was established that the entry had been forced through a back window on the ground floor. The thief had touched nothing on his way up to the first floor, though if he had

166

taken his time he could have found some quite choice items in two of the lower rooms. It must have been a nervy, spur-of-the-moment break-in, which would make it all the harder to sort out.

A SOCO, scenes of crime officer, was already at work on the window dusting for prints. There were distinct marks of a jemmy, but nothing in the way of dabs or even glove marks.

Galloway groaned. They had scores of cases like this every month; but this time there had to be a perishing peer involved, didn't there!

Lord Barstow-Smythe surfaced at last with a photograph of the necklace.

'What theories do you have at the moment, inspector?'

'Could have been some kids, I suppose. Then again it could have been someone wanting it to look like that.' He was unable to take his eyes off the girl on the bed, festooned with gear which might have been rejected by Oxfam. 'Dreamy Lil over there,' he ventured: 'she couldn't have nicked it, could she?'

Something boiled up slowly within Barstow-Smythe. Galloway looked pale. Dave Litten had a feeling the guv'nor had gone a bit too far this time.

Barstow-Smythe let go suddenly and loudly. 'Cynthia? She couldn't nick her own fanny.'

Which seemed to settle that aspect of the case.

Litten was glad to follow the detective inspector out, gingerly holding the photograph and slipping his notebook back into his pocket. He had scribbled diligently in the book, but was well aware that the scribbles amounted to nothing of any consequence.

'Inspector!' Barstow-Smythe posed imperiously at the head of the stairs. 'It's imperative I have that necklace returned by the weekend. My mother will simply die if . . .' He let it fade away, accompanied by a limp wave of the hand.

'We wouldn't want to upset your mother, would we? No, rest assured, your lordship, we'll leave no stone unturned.'

Galloway, to Litten's relief, drove towards Sun Hill more

carefully than he had driven here. When they reached the station he did not get out, but motioned Litten to do so.

'All right, old son, now it's down to you.'

'To me, guv? Don't quite get it. I mean, shouldn't something like this be down to you?'

'I'm at court all day tomorrow, and there's someone I intend to see this very afternoon. Don't want any changes of plea or anyone getting washed down the sewers. So I've got to have someone doing the running about on *this* one, haven't I?' He wound his window down as Litten walked mournfully round the car. 'It's called delegating. You'll learn.'

'Thanks a lot, guv.'

'When I get back from court tomorrow I want to see those burglary reports on my desk, properly typed. Okay?'

Litten trudged on into the nick. He tried to persuade himself it was a good sign, him being given the responsibility of preparing all this. It showed what a good opinion the DI had of him. But typing was not his best point. He had looked forward to the CID as the branch where the action was, where the really complicated crimes got solved, and here he was filling in forms again.

The afternoon passed; his ashtray filled up with fag ends, and smoke curled round the filing cabinets; and still his typing showed no signs of improving. For the fourth time he crumpled up a sheet of paper and tossed it at the wastepaper basket – and missed.

Taffy Edwards stuck his head round the door some time in the early evening. 'How's the secondment to the superstars going, then?'

'I'm busy. Close the door behind you.'

'Nice piece of skirt at the front desk, boyo. Wants to see the man in charge. Told her Clouseau's gone home, I did, but his assistant, now . . . that, I said, is something else.'

Edwards made his escape before a ball of paper or even the whole wastepaper basket could be hurled at him.

Litten went out suspiciously to the desk. The smiling girl on the other side provided the most welcome diversion. She

168

was the first good thing that had happened since his transfer. Dark hair brushed the shoulders of her grey trench coat, and there was an inviting fleck of green in her wide grey eyes. The touch of her hand was cool, and she did not seem to mind it lingering in his for a few extra seconds.

'Jennifer Crosby,' she identified herself, 'from the *Herald*. You're DC Litten?'

'Yes, that's me.' But it was better to hedge it a bit. 'Well, sort of *acting* DC. Dave to my friends,' he added hopefully.

'I was told you could fill me in with a few details about Lord Barstow-Smythe's robbery?'

For all the demure smile and engaging tone of voice, she was businesslike enough when she took out a shorthand pad and pen.

Litten leaned nonchalantly on the counter. 'Yeah, well, it's a little bit hot for anyone round here to handle. You know what I mean? With an insurance tag like that – forty grand, I mean! – and easily identifiable . . . Probably halfway to Saudi by now.'

'Is there anything I can put down . . . Dave? Something to make up a few lines.'

She nudged the pad a little way across the counter, so that her hair fell down one side of her face and she was close to Litten, smiling a charming little plea up at him.

'Well, mustn't give too much away, of course. But how about . . . um . . . we expect an early arrest?'

The smile hardened a bit. Jennifer Crosby put her pad away. 'And I bet you got that straight out of Galloway's box.'

'You know Galloway?'

'Oh, yes.' She swung her bag over her shoulder and turned away from the counter. 'I know galloping Galloway all right. I've got an editor just as mean.' At the door she said: 'If you get anything interesting, do give me a ring, Dave. I have been known to buy the Old Bill a drink once in a while.'

Regretfully he watched her go.

It came as a pleasant shock next morning to find what a glowing little piece she had managed to write about him in the local paper. Skimming down it by the kiosk outside the tube station, he felt a rush of pride. This was the real thing, this was. Things moving, people depending on you, hanging on your every word. Rolling the paper carefully so there would not be too many creases across the more important parts, he strode into Sun Hill police station.

Jimmy Carver and June Ackland were in a huddle over the desk. They looked up and greeted him with silly smirks as he made his way purposefully through the open flap.

'Who's got his name in the paper, then?' said Carver, closing a ledger with a thump.

'All part of the job, isn't it?'

'Litten of the Yard!' sniggered Ackland.

Disdainfully Litten went to the radio desk to pick up overnight messages from the CID bin. At least this was real police work, not like going round sticking tickets on everything that moved. ~ or didn't move

'And if I were you,' said Sergeant Cryer from the far corner, 'I'd start dusting my helmet. Because when Galloway finds out you've elbowed him out of the headlines, there'll be hell to pay. Officer in charge, indeed!'

They were jealous, that was all it was. Litten left them and shut himself away contentedly in the CID office. He began to go through the messages and then, covertly, cast a glance at the folded newspaper; and unfolded it.

The phone rang.

The caller seemed a long way away, or might have been shielding his mouth with a paper, or half turning away from the mouthpiece. Throatily he said: 'Detective Constable Litten?'

'Litten speaking.'

'You don't know me, chief, but I've heard you're a fair man.'

'Who is this?'

'Never mind that, chief. Just listen a sec. How would you like to get your hands on that piece of tom from the Harvey Street job?'

'Too right I would. But who – '

'Meet me in the park, by the pond. Ten minutes, all right? But on your tod, or there's no deal.'

Before Litten could ask how he would recognize his informant, and even which park he was talking about, the dialling tone was ringing in his ear.

When he looked at the map on the wall there was little doubt about the park, anyway. There was only the one within a few minutes' walk. Still there was the matter of identifying the man when he got there, or of being identified. Then he got it. The newspaper lying on his desk – that must have given the man his name. Where else would he have picked it up?

Litten tucked the paper under his arm and dashed out of the office.

The park was almost deserted at this time of the morning. A few kids were playing and screeching in the distance, and the ducks on the pond were kicking up one hell of a fuss, but otherwise there was only one person in sight. Litten quickened his pace along the path which led to a rustic shelter and on down a brief slope to the water's edge. A man with a flat tweed cap crushed down over his ears and forehead was tossing pieces of bread to the clamorous ducks.

Litten halted beside him, uncertain. The man wore a pseudo-military raincoat over a blue blazer, with a badge on its pocket which implied a lot without actually saying anything. He did not acknowledge Litten's presence for a moment but went on tossing the last remaining crumbs into the pond. Then from the corner of his mouth he said:

'Come alone, did you, chief?'

'Just as you said.'

'Funny things, ducks.' The man dusted a few fragments off his hands. 'Only want you when there's something in it for them. Like people, I suppose.'

Without warning the stranger began to saunter along the path bordering the water. The ducks formed a flotilla to pursue him.

'The jewellery,' said Litten. 'You said on the phone you knew where it was.'

His companion shook his head. 'Oh, no, I didn't say that, son. You Old Bill, always wanting to put words into people's mouths.'

'But you did say – '

'Not me, son. What I *am* telling you is that I can find out. Now that's a different kettle of fish, isn't it?' Just as Litten began to feel that this was a washout, the man went on: 'You're looking for a couple of youngsters.'

'We are?'

'Can't get rid of it. Nobody wants the aggro. Haven't got a clue, the silly little sods. Probably throw it in the canal, they will.' He looked genuinely shocked.

'You know who they are, where they hang out . . . anything?'

'Gotta be an earner in it for me, chief. Nothing for nothing, know what I mean? If I'm going to put myself out, I want some real money. Like today. Insurance money.'

Litten was out of his depth. But he remembered some of the training and some of the principles they had dinned into him. 'Insurance companies are a bit iffy on things like that. Pay out rewards on conviction only.'

'Want that bit of tom back, don't you? See those villains up before the beak, get your bit of glory. Detective Litten cracks it!'

'Yeah, but – '

'Look, insurance people are businessmen, aren't they? Lay out a grand, get forty back. Just you have a word with them, and you'll see.'

'I don't know,' said Litten wretchedly.

By the time the little man had finished instructing him, he did know. But it was not something he wanted to tackle on his own. Why did Galloway have to be in court this morning of all mornings? He made his way back to the nick half sizzling with the prospect of maybe pulling off something good, and half chilled by nerves.

Sergeant Roach was in his usual place by now, and Dashwood was bustling to and fro.

'Sarge,' said Litten thankfully, 'I need a – '

'You need a good kick up the arse. It's ten thirty and the messages haven't been filed, you haven't booked on, and the uniform's screaming for – '

'Look, sarge, I need your advice. Urgently. It's about an informant.'

Roach lit a cigarette and tilted back in his chair. 'Watch it, lad. Have you looked it up in the good book?'

Litten had no need to look it up. He knew. It had been plaguing him all the way back. The training manual was designed to cover every aspect of the game, and one of its unforgettable rules from Chapter 23 – Litten could even see the page in his mind's eye – was that an informant was a dangerous breed, to be treated with extreme caution.

'This is something different,' he begged. 'I'm asking for your help.'

'Nothing's ever different. If it is, you'll have to find your own help. You don't like the responsibility, you shouldn't have applied.'

It was clear that Sergeant Roach had either had another row with his neighbour, or was giving himself ulcers with the effort of not having a row with his neighbour.

Litten tried to grab Dashwood as he passed, but Dashwood was muttering feverishly to himself. 'Second time this week that bloody solicitor's changed the appointment.' The mutter became a roar. 'Do get out of the bloody way, will you?'

He was snatching up papers and a briefcase, and heading for the door.

Roach was on his feet. 'There's a few jobs down to you in the book, Litten. Better sort yourself out before Galloway gets back.'

Then Roach, too, was gone.

Dave Litten collapsed into his chair. The whole thing was in his lap. Either he could play it safe, doing the odd jobs he had been left by Sergeant Roach, and telling the informant

173

when he rang that he would have to wait, or he could do what he had been advised to do. Nobody could blame him for stalling and doing it the first way. But if that meant losing the jewellery . . .

He had until midday. The man would be phoning then.

At eleven o'clock he gave in, and reached for the phone himself. According to the file on the case, the City and Global Insurance Company were responsible for covering Lord Barstow-Smythe's property – with the possible exception of Cynthia, thought Litten.

He was put through to a Mr Winstanley, and explained the position. It was not easy. Mr Winstanley sounded more hostile than anyone ought to sound when talking to the police. Litten tried to smooth it over, and to hurry a decision along. The company wanted to stall, just as he had thought of stalling. Of course it was against their company rules to pay out what was in effect a bribe to someone with criminal contacts, and to pay it out before they had even been assured of getting what they wanted in exchange. Equally, though, could you expect an informant to hang about waiting for maybe twelve months for a case to be wrapped up, the goods recovered (if they were lucky) and a conviction obtained?

'It's no skin off my nose, Mr Winstanley, if this geezer gets it into his head to ring his lordship direct.'

It came out more snappishly than he had meant, but it did the trick. He could almost sense Winstanley twitch. He began to feel optimistic and to forget his doubts. It was going to work. He'd show those snide uniform sniggerers out there a thing or two.

When the midday phone call came, right on the dot, he was ready for it.

'You've got yourself a deal,' he said in answer to that throaty voice.

'Right, chief. Now listen, I'll ring back within the next couple of hours. Maybe I can get back to you quicker than that. But you stay right there, and you'll be hearing from me.'

'I'd better.' Litten tried to assert some authority.

'I'll only say it once. The time and the place. Just once, get it? Then it's down to you.'

The time turned out to be two-thirty that afternoon. The place was a street of Victorian terraces which could have been as smart as Lord Barstow-Smythe and his neighbours' houses but had not yet been taken up by any fashionable set. Doors and windows had been boarded up, not smartened up. Bedraggled curtains still hung behind a few dusty panes. One whole segment had been marked for demolition. Some basement doors were secured by rusty padlocks. Others swung despondently on their hinges.

Litten, backed by two uniformed constables, trod carefully down a green-stained flight of basement steps. This was the place – unless it was all a hoax. That was what scared the daylights out of him.

There was a chink of metal inside, and a murmur of voices.

'Right.'

He thrust hard against the door, and it gave way before him. Light streaming in through the door and less brightly through the curtained window fell on two youths stretched out on a mattress – one reading a comic, the other beginning to open a sports bag and reach inside.

There was a jemmy in his hand and a bewildered expression on his pasty face as Litten triumphantly, mockingly said: ''Allo, 'allo, 'allo. What 'ave we got 'ere, then?'

Seventeen

Pride of place in the charge room was given to the necklace, spread out for everyone's inspection on the desk. Dave Litten smiled graciously as compliments showered around his ears. Sergeant Cryer, dourly keeping his distance from all the jubilation, went at his usual methodical pace through the list of items taken from the less spectacular sports bag. It made a pretty imposing total: a black rubber torch, a pair of gloves, a jemmy, one hacksaw, one chisel.

'Look, sarge,' implored one of the two lads, shoulders sagging, 'I don't know what you dragged us in here for. That gear's got nothing to do with us.'

His mate was shivering. 'Honest, I don't believe this is happening. Look, can I at least go to the toilet?'

'Hoping to flush something down the loo?' suggested Taffy Edwards. 'I'm wise to all those tricks, boyo. Haven't spent all my life down the pits, you know.' He held the boy with his left hand and ran the right one exploratively down his thigh.

'Look, I'm going to wet myself in a minute if you don't stop messing about.'

Past the rest of them, Litten saw Detective Inspector Galloway come in from the outside world and survey the scene in wonderment.

'Hello, guv. Glad you got back.' Litten shouldered his way towards his boss. 'Tried to get in touch, but – '

'Had it off, then, Litten?'

'Had a bit of luck, as it happens, guv.'

Galloway looked at Cryer and the collection of tools, and at the gleaming necklace. He pursed his lips. 'Well, better come upstairs and tell me all about it, my son.'

They went through the outer office and on into Galloway's room. Without another word, Galloway tossed his raincoat over a spare chair and took off his jacket.

'Must have tried a million times to get through, guv,' said Litten placatingly.

'Close the door.'

'Did the best I could. Used my initiative, like you've always told me.' He didn't like Galloway's predatory expression, as if he were waiting for one little mistake he could pounce on. 'Put myself in your position, guv. Tried to think like . . . well, you know what I mean . . .'

Galloway pointed a threatening finger, then grinned. 'It looks like you did well, my son.'

'Phew, guv. You really put the – '

'But I'd like to have been put in the picture a little earlier. I don't like to be the last to know. Remember that!'

'Yes, guv.'

'Now, make yourself comfy. And let's go right through it, right from the beginning. Right?'

Litten crossed his legs. Confidence was surging back through his veins. His judgement had been right. Galloway was in a mood to be pleased with results.

Airily he said: 'You know how it is, guv. Put the word out on the streets. Got in touch with a couple of my snouts. Word soon got round.'

'Snouts?' said Galloway dubiously. 'Didn't know you had any, Dave.'

'Well, I don't like to put it about. He's a bit sensitive. You know what I mean. Might not get on the blower if you don't . . .' He became uneasily aware that Galloway was not even looking at him, but staring past him, over his shoulder, at something beyond the glass partition. 'So anyway, I leaned on him a bit . . .'

Behind him the door opened. Dashwood's voice said: 'Excuse me, guv, there's a Mr – '

'Winstanley?' said Galloway very quietly.

'Yes, guv. Actually, he's here to see – '

'I know who he's here to see. Ask him to wait.' As the door clicked shut again, Galloway got up very slowly. Light through the venetian blinds behind his head gave him a sinister halo. Litten could hardly see his expression, and was not sure he wanted to. 'Listen, my old son,' said Galloway venomously, 'and listen good. If you thought for one moment I was so naïve as to believe that load of – '

'Guv, I can explain.'

'Shut up and listen. One chance you've got, and one only. Now let's have it straight. No more of that crap you've been feeding me. Because if what's happened is what I think has happened, then you and that insurance man out there are in big trouble, believe me. *Tell me!*'

Litten gulped, and told him. Galloway nodded a couple of times, but it was not a nod of approval. When Litten had finished, he simply said:

'Let's go downstairs.'

A cell door was opened, and they were admitted to the stark little space where one of the two young men who had been arrested was sitting on a bench reading a comic, just as he had been when Litten led the raid on the basement.

'On your feet, son,' said Galloway. When there was no response, he stamped forward and shouted: 'I said, on your feet, son.'

The lad's eyes narrowed, and he half raised one arm as if to ward off a blow. Then he got up and stood in front of Galloway, staring defiantly.

Galloway said: 'There's only two ways you're gonna get out of here, my son. The choice is yours. It could be tomorrow morning by prison van, with so many charges round your neck they're going to throw away the key – understand? And that, sunshine, is when reality comes. When you meet all those other strong, silent types on remand, like yourself. Only they ain't silent any more. They're screaming the place down, protesting their innocence. Like you will be. But nobody listens. Nobody cares. Everybody's heard it all before, and it's too bloody late by then, my son. Too bloody late. D'you hear?'

The youth still tried to out-stare him, without a flicker; but he swallowed noisily.

Galloway dropped his voice. 'Now, listen. I know how you feel. You've been set up. I know that. But if you believe for one minute that there's honour amongst thieves, and it's up to you to stick by the rest of them, you're a mug. There's a lot of people out there doing time that'll tell you that – when it's too late.' He paused, and then said very gently: 'All I want, young man, is the truth. Nothing else.'

There was a long silence. Litten thought the DI would lose his temper and break into some sort of yelling match, but Galloway was holding off, waiting.

At last the youth said: 'The geezer said he wanted some decorating done. Said he 'ad a grant from the council.'

Bit by bit it came out. The stranger had come up to them in a café behind the buildings, and got into conversation. He wanted some work done on his old house – falling to bits, and there was a council grant, but only if he got started right away. He was getting on, had a bad back, couldn't tackle the job himself, but he was willing to pay out forty quid a day for someone who'd get cracking right away. They fell for it. He seemed straightforward enough. Gave them the address, told them to get round there and not be late, and he would bring the brushes and paint. The basement door was open, and the place certainly looked as if it needed doing up. They had settled down to wait for him, and then found that sports bag and wondered if there were some decorating materials in it . . . and then found the police on their necks.

'And that's the lot?' said Galloway.

'That's it.' The lad wasn't even expecting to be believed.

Galloway snatched the comic from his hand and led the way out, along the passage to the next cell.

The second lad looked up sullenly and said: 'Going to beat me to death with the *Beano*?'

Galloway showed every sign of doing just that. Instead, he

179

leaned against the wall and tapped the comic rhythmically against his knee as he began to go through the same routine, the same threats and same coaxings, until the same story began to emerge.

Both versions were on the same lines; and both were convincing. Wretchedly, Litten found himself believing every humiliating word.

He was hustled back to the CID offices by Galloway, who hardly deigned to nod to the waiting, nonplussed Winstanley from City and Global. He went through to his inner office, waved Litten in, and slammed the door with enough force to raise a squeak of protest from one loose pane of glass. As Litten watched, fearing that the worst could only get worse, he tugged open the top drawer of the metal filing cabinet in the corner.

'Right.' A folder was tossed on the desk under Litten's eyes. 'Read that.'

Litten studied the name on the front. It meant nothing to him. James Roland O'Hara had never yet crossed his ken.

Or so he thought, until he began to read.

The photograph showed a youngish face, but even with the addition of a small moustache and a tweed cap tugged down over the forehead Litten had little difficulty in recognizing it. It was a knowing sort of face. The report beneath showed just how knowing. O'Hara was a dangerous informant. His special method was seeking out young, inexperienced officers, tendering bogus information, and then claiming insurance rewards by setting up innocent youngsters with stolen property he himself had been unable to place. There were several other names at the foot of the evidence: O'Hara had been variously known as Captain Rowlandson, John Jackson, and even Jacob van Riet from Amsterdam. The names changed, the technique was unvaried.

'Do you realize,' said Galloway, 'how close you are to conspiracy to pervert the course of justice – you and that insurance man out there? Oh, you could get your name in the papers, all right!'

Dave Litten surrendered as abjectly as the two lads down in the cells had done. 'Guv, you've got to do something. I wasn't to know he – '

'There's two things going for you, my son. One is, at least you got the gear back. The other is, I know O'Hara. I know how his mind works.' He glared mercilessly at Litten, then allowed himself a grin with just a fleeting touch of sympathy to it. 'All right. What time's the meet?'

'Four o'clock,' whispered Litten, 'in the park.'

'By the pond?'

'Yes, guv.'

Galloway nodded as if he could have predicted this and every other move in the game.

'I think it's time I renewed my acquaintance with Mr James Roland O'Hara.'

Litten kept his head low as they went downstairs and past the main office. Sergeant Cryer tried a cheery wave, but did not seem all that surprised when there was no response. Taffy Edwards, coming out of the washroom, was on the verge of saying something, but decided against it.

'Guv, if he gets a whiff of you being with me – '

'He's not going to get a whiff. Forget me. Pretend I don't exist – the way you've been doing from the start of this brilliant deal of yours, right?'

They took separate routes to the park. Litten had no idea just where and how Galloway would surface, but that was none of his business. He had been given his own instructions and did not have to deviate from them. It was a load off his mind. From now on, whatever happened would be none of his fault.

He tried to walk easily, loose-limbed, as if he was still in charge. If O'Hara was lurking somewhere along the way, checking on him as he approached, there should be no grounds for suspicion.

Somebody waved to him across the street. It was WPC Martela, escorting some old biddy of the headscarf-and-curlers brigade towards Sun Hill. Litten was conscious of a

181

pang of envy. It was all right for that lot, wheeling in some tinpot shoplifter or fine-dodger, or listening politely to a tale of woe about a disappearing husband or a neighbour who kept stoking up a bonfire to ruin the washing, or happily leaning on a lorry driver whose tailboard had proved remarkably loose over the last few weeks. Child's play, provided you did it strictly according to the book. Money for jam.

He braced himself as he reached the park gate. In the distance, through the ornamental shrubbery and the knotted trunks supporting the rustic shelter, he saw a lone figure standing by the pond, feeding the ducks. Given the chance, he would happily have gone right up to O'Hara and pushed him in. But he followed orders, working his way inside the park railings towards a clump of bushes by one of the paths leading to the shelter.

Through the foliage he glimpsed O'Hara tossing away his last handful of crumbs and looking guardedly around.

Nothing moved.

O'Hara took a few steps up the slope and settled on one of the lumpy seats at the corner of the shelter, from which he could see across the pond and along the main pathway.

He could not see the branch path which came right up behind the timbered building. Litten, tensing, saw Galloway walk swiftly and silently along the path and lean over the back of the seat.

'Up to your old tricks again, Jimmy boy?'

O'Hara shot up from the seat. He hardly glanced at Galloway, but began to run. Galloway did not bother to pursue. He waited, hands in pockets, as O'Hara belted up the path towards the gate.

It was Dave Litten's chance of redemption. This at least he had to do properly. He waited until O'Hara was in range, then launched himself from the bushes. It was a perfect tackle. They slid off the path and along the grass, and finished up with Litten sitting astride the crumpled little man, reaching to pluck a primula from the border and waft it across O'Hara's nose.

Eighteen

Mopping up the tide of pornographic books and magazines was a job almost as unsavoury as the stuff itself. No copper worth his salt ever enjoyed posing as a member of the public and trying to con shifty dealers into digging something special out from the back room just in order to nick him. Of course the stuff was filthy and could turn your stomach when it didn't merely make you laugh, and there was a fair chance it did some damage to already diseased minds; but suppressing it was not the sort of thing that made you feel brave and virtuous.

So there was no great rejoicing when Jimmy Carver and June Ackland returned to Sun Hill with one Rodney Clements, on a six-month suspended sentence for stealing from cars and now caught doing that very same thing. His version of the story was that he had picked up a briefcase in the street and was on his way to Sun Hill to hand it in. In view of his remarkable turn of speed when he spotted the two of them, Carver and Ackland thought it more reasonable to suppose that he had lifted it from a parked car. The trouble was that the street in which they had intercepted him was jammed every day with commuters' and tradesmen's cars nose to tail along both kerbs. And another trouble was that Clements, on a 'suspended', was never going to admit to having even brushed against a parked vehicle. He stuck to his story: he had picked up the case in the street and hadn't the faintest idea what it contained.

When opened, it was shown to contain an expensive Nikon camera, a pocket calculator, a pair of sunglasses, and a dozen 'girlie' magazines. They were strong stuff, but not so strong

183

as to involve the owner in any trouble – whoever the owner was.

Also, however, there was a small blue notebook.

Sergeant Roach took charge of that, flipped through some of the addresses, and compared them with one of his files. A pattern began to emerge. Several of the phone numbers were those of newsagents who went on the defensive the moment Roach rang them. Some were on the other side of town. One was continually engaged, another did not answer. But whatever the connection was, it could be more important than just the magazines in themselves. Until they had more to go on, though, it was difficult to think of the next move. Maybe there wouldn't be any next move, unless somebody else was the first to make it.

The somebody else announced himself at the desk as a Mr Greenfield. He had lost his briefcase, and was most impressed to learn that the police had already recovered it. His lean, sallow face did not change hue when the magazines were laid out before him by Sergeant Roach. They were his personal property, along with the camera and the sunglasses and the rest of it. Nothing to be ashamed of, so far as he was concerned. But his eyes covertly sought something else as Roach counted out the briefcase's contents item by item.

It was not going to be possible to stall for ever. The man might have a grubby mind and a slimy manner, but he had committed no offence. It might all be open and above board, after all.

'Now, Mr Greenfield – '

'Sampson!' It was Roy Galloway, coming down the stairs and stopping suddenly, accusingly.

The man turned colour this time, and not a particularly attractive one.

'Sampson?' Roach echoed, bemused.

'You aren't being taken in by this con man, Ted? Dear old Eric Sampson – still into the perversities and the mucky lucre, eh?'

'Mr Galloway, I've done nothing wrong. Those books are for my personal use, and – '

'D'you think I've just stepped off the boat or something? Let me tell you, old son. When Sergeant Roach has finished checking out all the names and telephone numbers in that little book of yours and they tell me what I want to know, I'll kick your arse all round the charge room for wasting police time. D'you hear me?'

'But Mr Galloway – '

'Carver,' barked Galloway, 'search him. Then bang him up. Don't miss a thing. Make sure he's carrying nothing. I don't want him committing suicide. That's too easy a way out for this man!'

Bob Cryer looked dubiously across the room. Galloway was going it far too strong. But there was no stopping him now.

'Can I have a glass of water?' whimpered Sampson.

'No. You tell me where you've stashed the bulk of those magazines, and where you've been getting them from, then we can talk about favours.'

'Look, all I did was buy some from a man in the street. How can I be expected to know – '

'Imports from Sweden. Illegal imports, on a bet. And you wouldn't be in it unless there was a lot of money.'

'I lay odds you wouldn't believe your own mother, Galloway.'

'I'll tell you why I don't believe *you*, Sampson! Four years ago, West London, a lot of ordinary people lost their life savings. And you lost nothing. Quite the opposite. Right, Carver – finished? Then bang him up.'

As Jimmy Carver led the protesting, trembling man away, Bob Cryer said dubiously: 'You had me worried, Roy. I thought at one stage you were going to jump across and grab him by the throat. And I'm not so sure about all the "Dirty Harry" act. He might call your bluff.'

'But I've got the advantage, you see.'

'How come?'

'He suffers from claustrophobia,' said Galloway icily, 'and he's never been banged up in a cell before.'

Cryer looked even less happy.

Maurice Cohen had nothing to be happy about. The day had started out well enough, with the latest consignment arriving on time without mishap, and young Gary setting to work shifting the boxes into gaps already made in the avenues of waste-paper bales. Everything going smoothly, just the way it had gone so many times before. The fork-lift truck lifted the boxes labelled as *Holiday Brochures* from the lorry and dumped them neatly, then lifted bales across to cover them again. It was like music, the way it went so sweetly.

Then the phone had rung.

It was Eric Sampson. His briefcase had been taken from the car. He had got back just in time to see some young thief clutching it and being jumped on by the police. And it had his notebook in it.

Cohen mopped his brow. The music was going sour on him.

'Maurice, are you there?'

'I'm having a coronary, that's all. They've got the samples – and the notebook?'

'Maurice, it's not my fault.'

'Next you'll be telling me they have this number.'

It was only a whisper in the receiver. 'Yes.'

Cohen wanted to pinch himself so that he could wake up. This couldn't be happening, not after things had been organized so nicely. Sampson was too nervy for this kind of work, he'd always thought so. But he had to be stopped from panicking right now.

'Listen,' he said urgently. 'They don't know what they've got. And even if they suss it out, we've got maybe a couple of hours to move the consignment. So you go along there and reclaim that briefcase, and if they play awkward you demand your rights and ring our friend Sharman. Just stall long enough, right?'

186

Through the door into the warehouse he saw Gary scratching the angry red boil on his chin before manoeuvring the fork-lift into position again at the rear of the van.

'Hey! Start loading those boxes back on to the van, and move. It's a crisis.'

'But Mr Cohen, I'm halfway through getting 'em *off*.'

'When I say it's a crisis, it's a crisis. I'm paying you, ain't I?'

'You're driving me round the bend,' protested Gary, 'that's what you're doing.'

'Can't you work and complain at the same time? You're wasting precious time, and time I can't afford. So get moving.'

Gary swung the fork-lift angrily back towards the opening between bales. He went at it with such rage and frustration that one of the boxes swung out across the floor and burst against the jamb of the main doors out on to the street. Maurice Cohen squealed and ran forward, gathering the contents up in his hands and tossing them hysterically into the van. Not until the other boxes had been shovelled in any old how and Gary had heaved down the roller shutter did he feel he could breathe again.

'Right, Mr Cohen,' said Gary. '*Now* where do I take it?'

'To the police station.'

Gary stared. 'You don't mean you're going to hand over all that – '

'Hand it over? You think I give them presents, this time of year? Or any time of year? No, you park it outside, just the way I say. Listen . . . and listen good . . .'

Gary listened. At first he showed signs of wanting to cop out of this crazy idea. Then he laughed, and laughed a bit louder. 'Couldn't be much safer, could it? Until we're ready to collect.'

Even in the middle of this crisis, Maurice Cohen felt a spark of warmth towards anyone who could sound that admiring. Not that the kid wasn't right, of course.

He said: 'And when you're sure it *is* safe, you ring me, all right?'

It was a relief to see the van roll out on to the street and away towards the main road. It would be an even greater relief when he heard from Eric Sampson that the case and its contents had been safely removed from under the noses of Sun Hill police.

There was plenty of routine work to be done, but he was in no mood for it. The waiting was killing him. Maybe he should have stayed with the waste paper and steered clear of the glossy magazines.

No. It would come out all right. Everything had always come out all right for Maurice Cohen; though there had been one or two narrow shaves, and one or two people he was in no hurry to meet again.

At last the phone rang.

It was Gary. 'Done what you said, Mr Cohen. Cleared it with the sergeant – told him I'll get a mechanic round before the day's out. Real nice he was!'

'All right, all right. So that's worked a treat. Like I told you.'

'But I've got some bad news, guv. They've nicked Mr Sampson.'

Cohen felt the receiver going damp and slippery in his hand. 'Nicked him? But what for – what charge?'

'Dunno. But from what I heard, he'd been given a right going over by someone called Galloway.'

'Galloway!' It came out as a sob.

Now Maurice Cohen knew he was in real trouble.

'Cohen?' cried Galloway. 'Maurice Cohen – running a waste paper warehouse?'

Ted Roach turned the open notebook towards him, and dropped a slip of paper on top of it, covered with his own scribbles.

Galloway was on his feet. The jerk of his thumb ordered Roach and Dashwood to shift. They clattered down the stairs. There was no squad car available, and Galloway wasn't going to whistle one in. He tugged open the doors of his own

yellow peril – yellow once upon a time, before the strains and
nodules of rust began to freckle it – and they all piled in. The
engine coughed twice, and Galloway revved it mercilessly
before reversing wildly out of the yard, narrowly missing a
van parked at the kerb.

'There must be hundreds of Maurice Cohens,' observed
Ted Roach when he had regained his balance. 'What makes
this one so special?'

Galloway slowed for traffic lights, gunned the engine,
cursed, and shot forward to the accompaniment of a shout
from two women still a third of the way across a zebra
crossing.

'I should have guessed. He's the slimiest, shrewdest con
artist you'll come across. He's done me up like a kipper so
many times. If I can get my hands on him this time, I'll . . .
I'll . . .' The car faltered, jumped forward, and coughed again.
'But let me tell you, within half an hour of dragging that man
into the nick there's always a bent brief on the doorstep
demanding to see his client. He must send out radio signals
or something.'

He cursed again. The clanging of a fire engine in the
distance grew louder, and a policeman was standing at the
junction ahead, holding up traffic. The engine rushed across,
turning the way Galloway was waiting to turn.

The smoke was billowing out of a roof only half a mile down
the road. Tongues of flame licked out and then shrivelled as
jets of water lashed back, and foam began bubbling across
the façade of the building. One engine was already there,
giving all it had; the second juddered to a halt and began
unreeling its hoses; onlookers appeared, as ever, from
nowhere, gloating as if at a specially devised fireworks
display.

'Tell me I'm dreaming.' Galloway crouched over the wheel
and swung his car, hiccuping, in behind a fire tender. 'This
isn't true?'

'Convenient,' said Dashwood.

'Convenient my arse! He's done me up again.'

He thundered on into the smoking, dripping mess of what had once theoretically been a waste paper warehouse. The heat and humidity would have brought anyone out in a dank sweat. Part of a ceiling had fissured, pouring water on to already saturated bales of ancient newspapers and packaging. Roach and Dashwood went squelching through the papery marshland in search of magazines, while Galloway concentrated on the fire brigade chief.

'Where d'you reckon the fire started – out here or in the office?'

'Right out here.'

'Arson?'

'Possibly.'

'Come on, chief. Something more definite. You found a can . . . anything?'

'I'd rather not say until Mr Cohen's here to say what he thinks might have happened.'

'Hans Andersen will have nothing on that!' said Galloway.

'It wasn't him that reported the fire, you know. Some woman going past saw the first puff of smoke and went to a phone-box. Public-spirited, you might say.'

Galloway grimaced. 'Must have been a shock to Cohen, all right. He expected the place to be burnt to the ground by the time you lot arrived – or me!' He padded over the mess, looking with disfavour at the partly charred, partly drowned mounds of newsprint. 'Tell me,' he probed, 'if there'd been a load of magazines stashed away here, hidden somewhere, would they have been completely burnt out? I mean, would they be charred to nothing by now?'

'No,' said the fire chief decisively. 'Have you ever tried to burn a magazine at home – on a bonfire, perhaps? To get rid of it completely you have to feed the fire page by page. Have a look – some of these bales round here are charred on the outside, but the centres are untouched, hardly scorched. If anything you're looking for was still here, it would be . . . well, still here. Most of it.' He wiped a spattering of rancid water from his ear. 'An insurance job, maybe?'

190

'You could say that. But not the kind of insurance you have in mind.'

Galloway went back to the car and waited for Ted Roach and DC Dashwood to finish their perambulation. None of it had offered much that he couldn't have guessed, if only he had started guessing a bit sooner. 'He's got more tricks up his sleeve than Paul Daniels,' he said with what might have been admiration if it had not been undiluted hatred.

Dashwood was sceptical. 'You mean he removed the magazines from the warehouse and then set fire to all the other rubbish, just to put you off the scent? I mean, he wouldn't go to all that trouble, would he?'

'Yes, he would. That's the kind of man he is. He'd like me to believe they all went up in flames and there's damn-all evidence now, so we might as well give up trying. But those magazines are about all right, *somewhere*. And a lot more of Mr Cohen's sleazy imports, all illegal. I'm telling you.'

The car, having managed a mile and a half without a burp, began to produce some unsavoury spluttering noises.

'D'you notice, guv?' said Dashwood. 'Every time you mention Cohen, you get this sort of . . . well, I reckon the car must be on his side as well.'

As if to confirm this, the car lurched, slowed, jolted, and began an odd progression of leaps, pauses, and lurches. That was it so far as Galloway was concerned. He had had enough. Human beings were bad enough, malevolent enough. A maverick motor was inexcusable. Time to trade it in. Right this minute.

The car did a U-turn in the middle of the road, veered left, and went at an angle towards an open wired gateway.

Clinging to his arm-rest, Roach said: 'Bernie's?'

'Bernie's,' said Galloway vengefully.

Bernie was delighted to see him. Bernie had a whole range of spotless vehicles to offer the inspector. Bernie was known only for quality goods – or so Bernie told Galloway, who had heard most of it before but knew that if Bernie let him down there were ways of getting even. A deal was settled. A dark

191

green Cavalier – a demo model, used only by an expert who'd known what he was doing – and such a pity the trade-in price for the inspector's old wreck could not be more handsome: but then, the car itself wasn't what you could honestly call handsome, was it?

Yes, Inspector Galloway would be back later. Yes, the Cavalier would be ready for him to drive away. No, it would not start having an epileptic fit every time he was on the verge of making an important arrest.

They limped back to Sun Hill, almost as worn out as the car, but buoyed up by the thought of what they could now bring to bear on the demoralized Eric Sampson. He was the weak link. Cunning and elusive as Cohen might be, his henchman was there, ripe to fall.

Galloway swung savagely round towards the yard and nearly hit the van that was still parked there. Swerving well out to avoid it, he nearly tangled with a sleek BMW pulling away from the police station. Mouthing an insult, he saw a face inside, and mouthed something much fouler. As soon as he had stopped the car he was out, up the ramp, along the passage.

'Who let that bastard out?'

Sergeant Cryer had obviously been ready for this for quite some little time. 'Rules and regulations. I had to bail him out, Roy.'

'My ace card? And you let him go, you let him walk out of that door!'

'His solicitor showed up. A Mr Sharman. All very correct, Roy. What could I do?'

'You could have held him for a few more hours, somehow. Any old how. Used any excuse.'

Cryer shook his head reproachfully. 'You know better than that. The man was going berserk, screaming the place down, slamming his head against the walls. And his brief in here demanding to see him. He hadn't been charged with anything, so there wasn't any way of keeping him. You're the man who put me on the spot – tell me what I could have done?'

Galloway's contemptuous glare suggested three or four possible answers, none of them complimentary; but he knew there had been no way of holding Eric Sampson once that Sharman character arrived on the premises. He remembered Mr Sidney Sharman. Remembered, too, one or two other clients of Mr Sharman's.

As Roach and Dashwood settled down into their chairs and looked around in the hope of some coffee appearing on the scene, Galloway said: 'So Sampson's away. And Cohen's done a bunk. When they get together, who d'you suppose will be offering them the best professional advice?'

Nineteen

Gilded lettering on a first floor window identified the offices of Sidney Sharman and Partners, Solicitors. There was no sign of movement within, but Galloway had no doubt whatsoever that a lot of talking and waving of arms was going on behind that window. He wouldn't have minded being a fly on it.

Ted Roach said: 'How can you be sure he's in there?'

'I can't.' Galloway hunched over the wheel, surly but sure. 'Let's just say I have to assume *something*.'

This was a reasonable enough assumption. Sharman and Sampson had left the nick only twenty minutes ago, just as the three of them got back from the fire. Sharman's BMW was round the corner, and right behind it was Sampson's Merc. They simply had to be in there, hatching a moody defence, and either Cohen was with them or they were waiting for him. Or maybe they'd soon be on their way to a rendezvous. Theirs was not the kind of business you talked over the trumpet.

From the back seat Dashwood leaned between Galloway and Roach. 'Is that him?'

Large and podgy as he was, Maurice Cohen could move swiftly and unobtrusively. He had emerged from a door below the solicitor's office and was halfway across the pavement, hailing a cab, before Galloway's attention was drawn to him. Without Dashwood, he might have missed him.

He turned the ignition key. The car whined, chugged to itself for a moment, and then faltered. Galloway gritted his teeth. Not this time, *please* not this time!

They were away. He kept the cab in sight with some

difficulty. Traffic cut across his eyeline, lights changed and he had to make a risky dash across them, and all the time he had to hang far enough back to ensure Cohen did not spot him. They were heading in a familiar direction, though. Cohen lived only a few streets ahead. If he kept to his usual MO, the cab would drop him at any moment and he would walk the rest of the way down a narrow cutting. That was when they would lift him. Galloway felt a tightness in his throat. This time he was not going to miss.

The cab was slowing and pulling in to the kerb. Galloway braked sharply, and tucked his car in behind a parked truck, sticking out far enough for him to see the back of the cab. Dashwood, head rammed against the window, peered over his right shoulder.

Instead of getting out on the pavement and walking to the cut, Cohen appeared in the middle of the road, dodging between traffic.

'The devious git!' said Roach. 'He's crossing back again!'

Galloway pulled out desperately, and began to veer towards their quarry. 'Straight in and grab him – and don't let go! If he gets the chance, he'll run like hell. And he can run!'

Cohen glanced to one side as the car passed him, worried for a moment. Then it pulled up sharp ahead of him, and Roach and Dashwood tumbled out. Cohen saw he really had something to worry about. It was true he could run. But Galloway swung round in the middle of the road, to a blare of indignant horns, and coasted along the wrong side of the road, stopping Cohen from making a break for it. Roach caught up and seized Cohen's arm. Dashwood, grabbing the other, wrenched open the back door of the car, and they threw him bodily in.

'So suddenly the Metropolitan Police go in for kidnapping?' panted Cohen. He slumped back. 'Maybe you want to caution me, eh? Maybe you want to say "Maurice, you're not obliged to say anything" . . . ?'

Which was virtually what they did say to him when he was safely installed to everyone's satisfaction in the charge room.

By then, even Cohen himself looked satisfied rather than frightened. He faced Galloway's questioning with a confidence born of long years of questioning and evasions, a sly knowledge of his rights and apparent innocence of any wrongs.

'You confuse me.' He looked genuinely hurt, yet anxious to help. 'You talk about fire. You talk about arson. You talk about burning the books, but what books? Are you talking about my VAT books, account books – '

'You know what books I'm talking about.' Galloway was unable to control himself. 'I'm talking about the ones you haven't burnt!'

'Maybe we are talking about library books? Ai, of course, I should forget so easily! No more than two weeks overdue, I promise you, inspector.'

Galloway saw red. Maurice Cohen certainly had something overdue, and he was going to rectify that. He seized him by the collar and began forcing that smug, moist face closer and closer to his own. Ted Roach shifted uneasily, moving his weight from one foot to the other.

'You're playing for time, you lousy little ponce. I'm warning you . . .'

The door opened and Sergeant Penny stuck his head round it. 'There's a Mr Sharman arrived. A solicitor. I've put him in the waiting room.'

'And let him bloody wait.'

But Maurice Cohen's face told him that this round was over, and the police had lost. You couldn't push things too far – not with a cunning brief like Sidney Sharman sitting out there counting off the minutes and framing more and more accusations against the CID and its methods. Galloway let go of the collar and stalked menacingly off to the waiting room, to be greeted by Mr Sharman's infinitely courteous, infinitely knowing smile.

'How is my client, inspector? Well, I trust?'

'Well trained.'

'That, I take it, means you're not getting very far with whatever it is you've trumped up against him?'

'You talk to me like that and . . .'

'And?'

'At the moment,' said Galloway stiffly, 'he's still helping police with their enquiries.'

'Come, come, inspector' – Sharman's smile broadened – 'you can do better than that.'

Galloway gave in. There was no point in prolonging the agony. 'All right, you can have him. But I want him and Sampson back here in a week, without fail.'

'You think by then you'll have enough evidence to lay charges? If not . . .'

Galloway knew well enough what that 'if not' implied. But to himself he swore he was going to have the evidence, and he would have them bang to rights, and there'd be no way Sharman was going to get them off. No way.

Cohen patted Galloway's arm as he left. It was a kind, consolatory pat. Galloway had half a mind to charge him with technical assault. But Roach and Dashwood were watching. They had already seen him nearly go over the top. It was not a good idea to create the impression that he was out of control, losing his grip.

Somebody was going to feel the strength of that grip any day now.

At any rate it was cheering, over an early breakfast, to be able to tell Maureen that today he was collecting a new car. She couldn't pretend she wasn't pleased: some of his worst outbreaks of temper had been due, these last few weeks, to breakdowns along the road and delays in getting home because the motor's temperament had been even more awful than his own.

He was in a tolerably good mood when he wheeled the old banger into Bernie's yard and took over the Cavalier. It did not cough, it did not stutter, and it didn't need revving ferociously every time you pulled away from traffic lights.

Nice handling, nice turn of speed, nice steering. He swung with some dash into Sun Hill station yard, and narrowly missed the van that had been parked against the wall.

'Morning, guv,' said Litten cheerily. 'That's a right tasty-motor you've got there.'

Litten's cheerfulness was the sort that could put a damper on your own good mood at the drop of a helmet. Galloway glowered his way into the front office.

'Who stuck that van in the yard? One day it's bunging up the street, the next it's a death-trap right on our own premises.'

Sergeant Cryer grinned up from the night duty occurrence book, acknowledging the characteristic rasp.

'Broke down yesterday. The driver promised to shift it, but then he rang back to say he couldn't get the engine part until today.'

'Should have had it towed away. And why shove it in our yard, anyway?'

'I had the boys manhandle it in this morning, knowing you were taking delivery of your new crate. Didn't want you to graze it,' said Bob Cryer affably, 'as you came down the street.'

'Bloody near went head on into it, where it is now.'

'Give it an hour or two. If the lad's not round here with his spare part pretty sharpish, then it's off to the pound with it.'

Galloway grumbled his way up to the CID office, where Roach and Dashwood were tossing to decide who bought the tea. They looked peeved when Galloway squashed the whole idea of tea. There was serious thinking to be done. The obsession with Maurice Cohen was bubbling up in his mind again. Those bastards had to be screwed down. He needed a plan of campaign, but hadn't a clue where to start. Cohen and Sampson would be sitting tight and mute now. Without a word from their bent brief they would not venture a move. And if they made no move, what move could the CID possibly make against them? It was a waking nightmare which was going to give Galloway no peace.

The phone rang. Dashwood took the call, then handed the receiver to Galoway.

It was Bernie. At the sound of his voice, Galloway flinched. It was all too likely that Bernie was already regretting the exchange price he had allowed for the old car, and was going to start haggling and accusing him of pulling a fast one.

Bernie said: 'You lost anything?'

'What sort of thing?'

'Like the keys to hidden treasure. Didn't know the CID had special accounts like that.'

'What the hell are you talking about?'

'Better come and collect them,' said Bernie, 'when you're next passing.'

A flutter of suspicion jumped at the back of Galloway's mind. It did not amount to anything much yet, but it could be quite something. He needed a lead. This could be a false one, but he wasn't going to let it rest until, as Bernie put it, the next time he was passing.

'All right, have your tea then.' He grabbed his jacket from the chair and shrugged it on as he passed Ted Roach.

On the edge of Bernie's forecourt one coloured lad was busily polishing away at a mildly dented bumper, while another stuck large plastic numbers on the windscreen. Roy Galloway looked incredulously at the price that was being asked for his old vehicle. Now he knew who had ripped off whom.

Bernie came bustling out. 'Hey, turn round, Roy. Be fair. You ain't supposed to see that. That isn't what you call, in the motor trade, etiquette.'

'You've got to be kidding.'

'When it comes to kidding' – Bernie turned them both away to face the blank wall – 'what's this about, then?' He unobtrusively drew a small leather pouch from his pocket and handed it over. 'Your Porsche account, is it?'

Galloway opened the spring mouth of the pouch to reveal two keys clipped inside. 'All right, where did you find it?'

'One of my lads cleaning out your old motor. He found it tucked under the back seat.'

'What did you mean by a Porsche account?'

'Oh, come on now, Roy. One of these keys on its own don't mean a lot, but two at a time, like that – well, that's a different story.'

It was true. Galloway turned them over on his palm and then clipped the pouch shut again. These were safe deposit keys all right. And who had been squashed into the back seat of that car who would have been likely to have a well-guarded deposit? Not Ted Roach or Dashwood, that was for sure.

'You're a diamond, old son,' he said gratefully. 'You have just made my day. Now all I've got to find, is *where*.'

Bernie sidled another couple of inches closer. 'You wanna know what bank? Now, it's only an idea, and don't ask no questions.' He tapped the side of his nose. 'No questions, understand?'

The bank manager viewed his visitor with some qualms, put his glasses on and then took them off again, as if uncertain which put things in the best light.

'I'd like to help,' he said dubiously.

Galloway plunged in. 'What if . . . look, say you simply go out of the office for a few minutes and leave the book open on your desk at the appropriate page? A sly glance, that's all I'll need.'

'You're asking too much. It's a breach of confidence to which I could not be a party. But as I've said, if the matter is as serious as you claim, I would like to help.' He sounded a mite more positive this time.

'Look, all I'm asking for at this stage is a name.' Galloway dangled the pouch between his fingers. 'The name that goes with this key, nothing else.'

'But it doesn't end there, does it, inspector? Once you have the name then you'll obtain a warrant for the deposit box to be opened – *if* you can get it – and you'll be back again.'

'But all these things take time,' begged Galloway, exasperated. 'What I need is a short cut.'

The manager shook his head. 'It puts me in a difficult position. You must surely appreciate that. On the one hand, I don't wish to see this bank being used as a custodian for illegal . . . well, whatever it may be. On the other hand, it is strictly laid down as a matter of bank policy . . .' He stopped, wrestling with what Galloway supposed to be his conscience. Galloway sat very still. At last the manager said: 'You have an idea who the key belongs to?'

'A little more than an idea. Otherwise I wouldn't be taking up your time.'

The bank manager got up and turned his back, staring with apparent concentration out of the window, although the view must be wearisomely familiar to him by now.

'To save us both embarrassment, inspector, I'm going to tell you something strictly off the record.' It sounded dry and distant, almost impersonal.

Galloway tensed. 'Off the record,' he repeated.

'Early this morning one of our clients, who will remain nameless, reported the loss of his keys. We do not at this bank, for obvious reasons, have duplicate keys. In such circumstances we arrange for the deposit box to be forced open in the client's presence. In the particular case I am talking about, the client wishes to remove some important documents urgently.' His fingers tapped a quiet tattoo on the window ledge. 'If you happen to be, shall we say, discreetly outside the bank about midday, you may be able to confirm your suspicions, Mr Galloway.' He turned back and put his glasses on again.

'And you would, of course, have a clear conscience.'

'I think I could live with that, yes.'

They smiled politely at each other, and shook hands. Galloway could not wait to get to a phone.

Twenty

Once again they were sitting waiting for Maurice Cohen. This time, though, they were taking no chances. There were two cars. Whichever way he went, one of them ought to be after him at a moment's notice. All the same, Roy Galloway had a nasty prickling sensation at the back of his neck. He knew the cause. It was sheer, downright fear that Cohen might have spotted them and taken his own evasive action, laughing his fat, foul head off.

Galloway reached for his handset. 'You're not too close, are you, Ted?'

It was Dashwood who replied. 'Sergeant Roach is out on foot at the moment, guv, having a quick shufty round the plot.'

Galloway swore. He had wanted both of them in the car. If Ted Roach got sussed out, he would murder him.

Suddenly it was Dashwood again. 'Guv, hang on. Cohen's arrived. He's pulled up in a cab, about five cars in front of me.'

Galloway wished he could see through the towering office blocks which loomed above him, or have some camera in that other car picking up and transmitting every move.

'He's going towards the bank,' said Dashwood. 'Should be in your view any moment.'

Galloway slumped down in his seat, but not so far that he could not see the entrance to the bank and the corner of the street opposite. A bus blocked the way for a few seconds. When it had gone, there was Cohen waiting to cross the road. Silently Galloway urged him on – on across the road, across the pavement, up the steps, and on into the bank. He ought not to be in there long. Galloway tried in his mind to follow him to a counter, to wait for the bank manager to come and escort him, for the two of them to go down however many steps there were to the vaults, for the gates to open and the deposit box be lifted out . . .

Was there a back entrance? He knew there wasn't – they had checked that most carefully – but still there was the prickling at the back of his neck, and still the chance that Cohen had something up his sleeve.

'He's out!' He pressed the handset close to his mouth as if Cohen might somehow hear him through the constant throb of the traffic. 'Looking for a cab. Right, Ted. Take him . . . *now!*'

The car surged out of the side street and headed for Cohen, waddling along the pavement. Some sixth sense alerted Cohen. Without looking round he ceased waddling and set off at a spanking pace, crossing the road, unaware that he was heading straight for the second car.

Galloway got out and stood complacently waiting for him.

Cohen, swinging a supermarket carrier bag in his right hand, seemed to let its weight steer him in a different direction. He must have a radar system like a bat's. With no obvious effort he was smoothly off the pavement and into the front door of a little Italian snack bar tucked between a tobacconist's and a wine bar which relied for its profits on the earnest wheeling and dealing of city businessmen.

'Watch it, mate . . .'

'I say, do look where . . .'

Galloway went in after Cohen, with Ted Roach thumping after him. Tables rocked with the impact of their hips. The proprietor, cutting and stacking sandwiches, looked up indifferently as if this sort of thing were normal in the world of banks, brokers, and top-hatted messengers.

Cohen was out of the back door well ahead of them. He hardly faltered, scanning the cramped road between the great stacks of glass and concrete, before launching himself into the turmoil of traffic. Again those weird antennae of his seemed to function independently of the highway code. Somehow he was on the far side of the street before Mike Dashwood had raced round the corner, converging on Galloway and Roach.

They finally pinned him down at a corner near a modern statue which, stooping over a hole in its own belly, looked marginally less afflicted than Cohen himself, dramatically massaging his chest with his right hand.

Neither his right nor his left hand was any longer in possession of that bulging carrier bag.

He surrendered to the three CID men with a pitying smile and no word of argument. The argument was left to Mr Sidney Sharman, who appeared at Sun Hill with an alacrity Galloway had to admire, if with a tang of bitterness.

The bitterness was enough to give anyone ulcers. Roy Galloway battered his desk with his fists until the windows rattled, and Roach and Dashwood wondered what decibel level had to be reached before you could complain to the noise abatement folk. Galloway had once more been forced to let Maurice Cohen go. There was no charge that could be made to stick. That plastic bag must have contained enough documented evidence in the way of accounts, foreign names and addresses, papers going back to the days when corruption was first invented, to put the bastard away for a minimum of three hundred years. But it had vanished without trace. Roach, Dashwood and two uniform men had retraced every inch of the route between where they picked him up and the bank. And there was nothing. There surely couldn't have been an accomplice they hadn't noticed, ready to grab the evidence and make off with it? Cohen must have ditched it, tossed it in some passing truck or dust-cart, rather than be caught with it in his possession.

Dashwood ventured: 'Even so, guv, we're still in with a chance if we can find out where those magazines are. The whole load must be around somewhere – they have to be.'

'Yeah, sure.' Galloway was despondent. Maurice Cohen had slipped through his fingers a few infuriating times before,

204

and obviously he had managed it again. 'What d'you reckon our chances are, then? Come on, you tell me.' He wanted to pace about the room and lay down the law, but the law wasn't in any helpful mood today. 'Those magazines,' he said, 'are placed some place we'd least expect them to be. A touch of the theatrical. Cohen's like that. Just to make us out to be bigger wallies than we already are.' He tried to blank it all out. 'Come on, let's go and have a cup of tea.'

They went glumly down to the canteen. At the desk, a young bloke in overalls was scratching a boil on his chin and saying unctuously: 'I'm sorry it took so long, sergeant. Can't tell you how grateful the boss'll be.'

'And you've got it started?'

'Like a dream, sergeant.'

'About time, too. Just get it out of the yard before I get into any more bother.'

The lad was digging into his back pocket. 'Can I put a quid in the poor box, or something?'

'The police orphans' box,' said Bob Cryer. 'And why not? It's the cheapest overnight parking you'll get anywhere round here!'

In the canteen, Roach and Dashwood collected their teas, and after a few sharp words about tea and milk slopped into his saucer, DI Galloway joined them. Roach winked and made a brief gesture towards a slumped figure alone at a table on the far side of the room. Dave Litten had his head down, either absorbed in contemplation or sunk in the depths of misery. With one accord they crept up on him. He had no warning until Mike Dashwood was sliding on to the chair beside him. Then he hastily dragged himself closer to the table.

Ted Roach's bushy eyebrows rose. 'What have you got there, Litten? Something you don't want us to see? Some promotional crib, or something?'

'Nothing, sarge. A magazine, that's all.' As Roach stuck out a searching hand, Litten blazed up. 'Leave it out, sarge. It's nothing to do with you.'

Roach grabbed the magazine and slung it down on the table. The cover was interesting, even at this time of day, even in this setting. From whichever angle they saw it, the three of them plus Litten, it was undeniably provocative: a girl up this way, another girl down that way, and a man with an expression which might have been greedy or just exhausted.

'Puts me off my digestive biscuit,' said Dashwood.

'I'm only browsing through it,' said Litten, going a fetching shade of pink. 'I'm over eighteen, aren't I?'

Galloway hunched over the cover as if to shield it from the delicate susceptibilities of two WPCs looking curiously across from their table. He said: 'You know better than to take anything out of the property store that's subject of an enquiry.'

'I didn't,' said Litten indignantly.

'Don't tell bloody lies,' said Roach.

Galloway took a mouthful of scorching tea. 'I'm not going to bollock you here, Litten. I want to see you, in my office.'

'I didn't take it from the property store.'

'Dropped off the back of a lorry, did it?'

'Funny you should say that, guv. I mean, it was like that, sort of. I . . . borrowed it from that van in the yard.'

'What van?' said Roach sceptically.

Galloway got that prickling sensation again, right the way down this time.

'The one that's broken down,' said Litten plaintively. 'I mean, there it was, sticking out – you know, trapped in the shutter as if . . . well, there it *was*. All I did was tug it out to have a look. Sort of.'

His mouth dropped open as Galloway, Roach and Dashwood deserted him with one accord. They went across the canteen like Olympic hurdlers, except that instead of leaping over the tables they knocked three of them aside and sprayed one wall with a bottle of tomato ketchup.

Galloway had been right. He had so often been right about Maurice Cohen, but it wasn't enough to be right about Cohen:

you had to outguess him before he had even started to set up whatever it was he wanted to set up. And who would ever have thought that he'd have the nerve to try one on like this?

The three of them shot out of the side door as the van rocked through the back gate, slewed left, and accelerated down the street.

Sergeant Cryer had let this happen. Sergeant Bloody Cryer had played into the hands of Maurice Cohen and made a laughing stock of Detective Inspector Galloway. Cryer would pay for it. Cryer was never going to hear the last of this.

Bob Cryer said: 'Another pint, Roy? Good for the stomach lining, they tell me.'

'Only a brewer would tell you that. Alcohol's just a slow destruction of the human body.'

'Who's in a hurry?'

They meditated over their tankards, while a juke-box started blaring in one corner, a one-armed bandit rattled behind them, and two youngsters leaning on the bar began to mutter together so intensely that they gave off an aura of pure villainy. It was so pure that any professional would know they weren't villains, not in a million years.

Galloway brooded over the thin film of froth sparkling on the surface of his beer. 'D'you know something? This is a mug's game.'

'What – drinking?'

'No, you berk. The Force. The job. Must be easier ways of earning a crust.'

'I reckon there is.' Cryer eyed the pint. 'Fancy a Scotch to go with it?'

'No, I'll have a gold watch.'

'Not yet you won't.'

They looked on the day just gone, and the weeks and months and years gone by. And the days and weeks and months and years lying ahead wouldn't be all that different. Maggie would be back with her tins of salmon – unless she decided to switch to tinned peaches. Mrs Draper's kid would be back, until he was too old to bother, and by that time some other little urchin would fancy the idea of chocolate bars in the police station. Breaking and entering would go on at a faster rate than the sun could ever manage to rise and set, and people's homes would be defiled, pawed over, making you so sick you wouldn't want ever to set foot in the places again.

And the demos. They came round as regularly as bank holidays and rainy summers. Peace protesters would go on walking into the massed ranks of patriots with knuckle-dusters and lurid armbands. Yobboes would roll marbles under the feet of police horses and shove bottles into the faces of football fans down for the day. Prime ministers of places you'd never heard of would come for a state visit, and every road would have to be sealed off even if there was no remote chance of any of them ever wanting to see these seedy streets and seedy people.

And every year there'd be some raving loony wanting to stage a street carnival.

Dirty streets, dirty books, dirty habits, dirty deals on every corner and behind a hundred dirty windows. Lost cars, lost hopes, women screaming they had been raped and other women going for their husbands with kitchen knives or lethal kneecaps. Lost property, larceny, lost beliefs . . .

Roy Galloway said: 'You ever thought of jacking it in?'

'About as many times as you, I reckon.'

In the distance the siren of a police car began to wail imperiously. They pricked up their ears; but stayed where they were. It might mean work for them tomorrow. This evening it was somebody else's pigeon.

'One of these days I'll just tell them,' said Galloway earnestly. 'Tell them to stuff it.'

'Yeah, that would be good, wouldn't it. Me an' all. A great day that would be. Why don't you stuff your job right up your arse, eh?'

Bob Cryer laughed. Roy Galloway laughed. They were talking nonsense, talking far-flung fantasy; and they knew it.